FRONTIER OF VIOLENCE

In 1962, the Indian army was fighting the Red Chinese along the North East frontier. The war was no business of British Naval Intelligence — until stolen British rifles were found on the battlefield. Paul Mason of Intelligence soon found that the arms were only a pawn in a much more complex game. Somewhere an evil mind was fanning the flames of war. The trails all led to an isolated monastery high in the mountains, and Mason's mission culminated in explosive violence.

CHARLES LEADER

FRONTIER OF VIOLENCE

Complete and Unabridged

LINFORD
Leicester

First published in Great Britain

First Linford Edition
published 1998

British Library CIP Data

Leader, Charles, *1938*–
Frontier of violence.—Large print ed.—
Linford mystery library
1. Detective and mystery stories
2. Large type books
I. Title
823.9'14 [F]

ISBN 0–7089–5266–6

Published by
F. A. Thorpe (Publishing) Ltd.
Anstey, Leicestershire

Set by Words & Graphics Ltd.
Anstey, Leicestershire
Printed and bound in Great Britain by
T. J. International Ltd., Padstow, Cornwall

This book is printed on acid-free paper

1

Stolen Arms

The night was made hideous by the crash and roar of heavy guns as they echoed resoundingly through the jagged ranges and mountain valleys. The scream of shells and the crunch of explosions split the black hell of darkness into a thousand shreds, tearing at earth and trees, stones and rock, and flesh and blood. Throughout the long night the endless assault went on and on, as though the world had gone insane with its own savage cruelty.

And then at dawn the big guns stopped. The first dull glimmer of cheerless grey silhouetted the majestic icy crests of the Himalayas soaring up to the roof of the world, and the sounds of battle ceased as though a giant sword had cut them short in one swift downward stroke through the chill air. Only dust and smoke stirred in

1

the flattened valley, and the silence was as grimly ominous.

It was literally the lull before the dawn, for before the grey had fully developed into first light the first wave of the Chinese invaders swarmed in a yellow avalanche along the path the artillery had cleared. They came across the Himalayan barrier from the lofty plateau of crushed Tibet, thrusting relentlessly through the high passes into Assam and India. The new day opened to the sharper echoes of rifle, machine gun, and bazooka fire as the first ranks of the desperately resisting Indian Army were overwhelmed.

Throughout the day the fighting raged fiercely across the rugged hills where India's North East frontier bordered with Chinese-occupied Tibet. By noon the Communist hordes had pushed the front line five miles to the south, and then hurriedly-rushed Indian reinforcements had checked the advance and gradually turned the tide. A desperate counter attack by the fresh Indian troops pushed the Chinese slightly back towards their original dawn positions, but failed to regain all the ground that had been lost.

At dusk the heat of the fighting diminished, the pressure easing by uncommunicated but mutual consent. Both sides dug in to secure their present positions and to lick their wounds until the war flared into full savagery once more. The artillery and mortar fire still continued, but much less heavily.

In the no-man's-land left vacant between the conflicting forces Lieutenant Panjit Sangh sprawled face down on the fire-blasted earth. His cap was missing and there was a bright trickle of blood leading from a slight gash behind his left ear. The cold, damp air soaked into his unconscious body and revived him slowly. He stirred and choked harshly as the dust and smoke that shrouded him stung inside his lungs. It took him several moments to realize where he was, and why he could only cough and choke instead of breathe.

The whine and crunch of a distant shell made him recall the shattering, earth-spraying explosion from a few feet away that had been his last conscious memory, and he sat up slowly. A scattering of tiny stones fell away from him as he moved and he realized that he had been showered with dirt. His uniform was filthy and one of his rank tabs was half torn away. He shook off another fit of coughing and then distinguished the shallow crater that had been made by the shell that had blasted him down with its close impact.

He wondered vaguely what had happened to the patrol that he had been leading. There were no other bodies around him and so he concluded that they had either retreated back to the Indian lines, or that they had continued advancing to annihilation. Either way they had left him for dead and he was alone.

The earth was damp beneath him now and he was shivering with cold. He stood up shakily and wished that the throbbing ache would clear from the back of his head. He was not yet aware that he had been wounded for he was attempting to concentrate his mind on his isolated position. He had no idea of where to find his own unit, or even of where to find the Indian front line. The sky was blacked out by cloud and there were no stars to provide any sense of direction. He shivered again and then remembered the wind that was cutting through him. The wind usually cut down through the Himalayan passes from the north. If he turned his back on the wind he would be heading south. He swallowed hard and moved off slowly, still coughing and stumbling with every other step.

The darkness was all but absolute, and apart from the occasional sound of shells he was alone in the night. He flinched each time he heard the whining note as one approached, but none came near him. The fact that they came from behind him and always exploded somewhere ahead strengthened his belief that the wind was guiding him back to his own lines, for most of the heavy artillery along the frontier belonged to the Chinese, they were the aggressors, whereas the Indians had been caught unawares.

He began to feel the first tugs of exhaustion as the cold night air curled around his weakened body and his head was pulsing horribly. At first he had attempted to remain alert for any sound that might indicate a Chinese patrol, but soon he was stumbling blindly in a near-helpless haze. He blundered down a barren slope and tripped headlong over a fallen body.

The Chinese uniform and the bared teeth in the sallow face made him scramble away quickly as he saw them dimly in the gloom. But the Chinese soldier was dead, and had been dead for some time, and after a moment the Indian Lieutenant was able to push down his first natural repugnance.

The Chinese soldier lay on his back with his face up to the sky. His cap with the emblazoned red star lay beside his head. There was red on the chest of his uniform and a rifle was still gripped in his outflung hand.

Sangh drew a breath and reached tentatively for the rifle. He had been holding his own revolver in his hand when the shell had knocked him out, and on recovering had been too dazed to think about it. Now the sight of the rifle

6

made him realize that he was unarmed.

The dead man's fingers had locked in death, and his grip was difficult to break. Sangh gritted his even teeth tightly together, but it had suddenly become imperative that he should arm himself before penetrating any farther across the dangerous no-man's-land and with an effort he wrenched the weapon away.

He sat with the rifle in his hands, the dead man forgotten as he stared at it. The very feel of it generated a strength of confidence that helped him to rally his fading determination. Now that he could defend himself he felt as good as home.

Then he noticed something that made him suddenly forget his own position.

The rifle in his hands was British.

He stared again, twisting the weapon slowly. He had trained with British weapons and there was no mistake. The rifle was of the latest pattern now used by the British Army.

But what was a Chinese soldier on the Himalayan frontier doing with British arms?

Sangh didn't know, and after a moment

his more personal problems again over-rode the importance of his discovery. The matter would have to be reported to his Commanding Officer, but meanwhile he would have to get back to his own lines. He rose to his feet again, gripping his newly acquired rifle across his chest as he left the dead Chinese behind him and continued wearily into no-man's land and the night.

★ ★ ★

Sixteen hours later, and two thousand five hundred miles away, Lieutenant-Commander Alan Kendall stood with his back to his large, air-conditioned office beneath Victoria Peak and stared out over the twin cities of Hong Kong and Kowloon. His eyes were creased against the bright glare of sunlight that struck through the window, but as he watched the junks and sampans manœuvring on the placid silver-blue dazzle of the straits the scene made only a dim impression on the outer surface of his mind. His inner thoughts were far removed from the island colony.

A door opened behind him and he turned without hurry to face the interior of the office, the headquarters of the Far Eastern division of British Naval Intelligence.

"Come in, Paul," he said quietly. "Don't stand on ceremony."

Marine Captain Paul Mason came in, closing the door behind him. He was above average height, but not quite six foot, and despite his service uniform he managed to carry an air of sporting, almost dandified elegance. Kendall knew that off duty Mason had a preference for casual clothes, bright open-necked shirts with a white silk cravat, and that he had the charm and lounging manner of a rich wastrel. Kendall also knew that despite the flamboyant touch to his nature Paul Mason was one of the best officers in the Marines, trained in Commando tactics, underwater sabotage, and a variety of other unlikely and dangerous skills. It was the double sides to his nature that made him such an excellent Intelligence man.

Kendall came away from the window.

"I don't suppose I need to ask what you found in Macao," he said calmly. "If the lead had been worth following you would have said so when I had you recalled."

Mason nodded. "Right first time, Commander. It was a false trail. Somebody ought to boot Fat Chung's backside."

Kendall grinned. "I've often thought about it. But the trouble with squeals and tip-offs is that sometimes they prove to be genuine, and you have to follow them all before you can be sure. But — " He became serious. "I think we can forget our friend Fat Chung and his false trails to Macao. The job has taken a new twist."

Mason's blue eyes fixed sharply on his senior officer's face.

"You mean there was another raid last night? Another arms store?"

Kendall shook his head. "No, Paul, a different development altogether." He gestured to the chair on the far side of his wide desk. "Sit down and I'll explain."

Mason sat down, resting his cap on the smooth mahogany surface in front of him. Kendall occupied his own chair and began grimly.

"As you know we've had three major raids on our Far Eastern naval bases in the past two weeks. One on the arms depot at Singapore and two here at Hong Kong. In each raid the thieves got away with a large haul of brand-new rifles, submachine-guns and thousands of rounds of ammunition. And in the last raid here we lost one naval rating, murdered on guard duty. Each raid was well organized and well executed and so far we have no idea of who was behind them. No one saw any of the raiders clearly, except perhaps for that poor devil who had his throat slit."

He paused for a moment, his jaw rigid and his mouth clamped tight. Mason remained silent and so Kendall continued.

"Losing the arms and having one of our men brutally murdered is bad enough, but there's another aspect of the business that has been worrying me even more. And that's the prospect of where those arms will eventually reappear, and for what purpose. I thought at first that they might have been destined for Indonesia, or Vietnam, but now it seems that I was wrong. The first of those missing rifles has turned up in the Himalayas on India's North East frontier."

Mason gave him an incredulous look. "The Himalayas! But how the hell could they get up there?"

"That's what I want to know. Last night an Indian officer lost himself in the no-man's-land where the heaviest part of the border fighting had been going on. He also managed to lose his revolver so when he found a dead Chinese the first thing he did was to help himself to the man's rifle. That rifle was one of ours, and after the Indian had found his way back to his own lines he reported the fact to his C.O. The C.O. also had a couple of other instances of the Chinese being armed with British rifles being brought to his notice, for they had managed to capture a few prisoners. There were three rifles in all and the serial numbers prove that they were part of the haul stolen in the raid on Singapore. At the moment the

Indians are making a bit of a stink about it, and I can't say that I blame them."

Mason said slowly. "But it doesn't make sense, Commander. Why transport arms all that distance when there must be ready markets so much closer. The transport problem must boost the price and I can't see the Chinese needing stolen arms that badly. In fact I can't visualize the Chinese bothering to get arms that way at all, even large consignments such as we've lost would only be a drop in the ocean for an army of that size."

Kendall nodded. "As you say, it doesn't make sense. But somehow we've got to make sense out of it. And by we I mean *you*. I've already got enough men covering the Hong Kong and Singapore ends, and if there is anything to be found they'll uncover it eventually. That's why I called you back from that wild goose chase in Macao. I want you to go up to the Himalayan frontier and tackle the case from there. The Indian Army Commander in that area has already agreed to assign you a liaison officer and he's also agreed to give you a free hand in interrogating those Chinese prisoners who were captured with our weapons. There's a naval aircraft laid on to fly you up to the battle lines."

Mason nodded briefly, with no more emotion than if he had just been ordered to take a slow train from London to Margate.

"I'll try and bring back something other than wild geese," he said calmly.

2

Ambush in the Mountains

Mason watched the Himalayas appear far to the north like gleaming, pointed islands of snow and ice in a blue-white sea of cloud and mist. Below lay the rain-soaked hills of Assam, cloaked in lush green tangles of bamboo and jungles. Down there the grass would be swampy underfoot, the matted vegetation would be sodden beneath the higher branches and black leeches would suck at the flesh of the unwary traveller. In the drier parts elephant and leopard roamed freely and it was possible that heads were still being hunted in the eastern Naga hills towards the frontier with Burma. Mason contemplated on the prospect and decided that he was glad the Chinese advance was still being held back in the mountains above the jungle line. He yawned and carefully closed his eyes. He had spent the best part of the last two nights prowling the back alleys of Macao, and although the long flight from Hong Kong had helped to make up his loss of sleep he saw no reason to waste the opportunity to get ahead.

An hour later a hand shook his arm. He was instantly awake, but controlled his eyelids so that they rose slowly and lazily. A young Flight Lieutenant grinned at him and released his arm.

"Sorry to wake you, Captain. But we've arrived. We'll be landing in five minutes."

Mason reached for his safety straps. As he did so he glanced through the window again where the huge range of peaks filled the skyline directly beneath the plane's wing.

"Thanks," he said. "But try not to hit one of those — they look fragile."

The Flight Lieutenant grinned again. "We're always careful. If we dent anything the Navy makes us pay for it — that's why we hate landing on aircraft carriers." He gave a brief salute and then returned to his place beside the pilot.

Mason relaxed again as they swept down towards the single airstrip that had been cleared among the mountain foothills. He watched the dusty earth rushing up to meet them and then with a gentle bump the wheels touched down. He unbuckled his safety straps but remained sitting until the plane had taxied to a stop.

Immediately two army jeeps came scurrying towards them, clouding dust from their speeding wheels, and by the time the fuselage door had been opened and Mason had dropped down on to the concrete runway both vehicles had screeched to a halt. Mason waited as a young officer swung nimbly out of the leading jeep and walked briskly towards him.

As he waited the Marine Captain's glance made a seemingly idle but thorough appraisal of the airstrip. It was a single runway across a narrow plain scooped out of the foothills. The surrounding ranges were barren and inhospitable, becoming beautiful only to the north where the peaks of the main range thrust above the snow line. There were a few hastily-constructed wooden buildings at the east end of the runway, a stationary Whirlwind helicopter, and a line of four Indian Air Force Dakotas like well-fed, fat-bellied birds. The airstrip gave the impression of having been hurriedly cleared and the control buildings thrown in as an afterthought. Mason remembered how the Indians had been taken by surprise by the Chinese attack and decided that the impression was probably correct. A week, or two weeks, ago there would have been nothing here but the empty plain. Even now the air was clear and peaceful and he wondered how far they were from the actual front line. Judging from the height he guessed that they could not be far.

He recalled his thoughts in good time to meet the young Indian officer. The man stopped and gave an elegant, fluid salute. He smiled in the same moment, showing off very white and perfectly even teeth of which he was obviously very proud.

"Captain Mason?" he said cheerfully.

"I am Lieutenant Panjit Sangh. I have been appointed to act as your liaison officer and aide."

Mason returned the salute and the smile, feeling vaguely self-conscious of a crooked front tooth that had been knocked slightly sideways six months ago in a Saigon bar. He had intended to see a dentist about that tooth but had never had the time. Now the Indian's gleaming smile was nudging his memory.

They shook hands briefly and then there was a short interlude of acknowledgements and introductions as Panjit Sangh turned his attention to the crew of Mason's plane as they assembled on the runway. The Indian finished by inviting them all to the officer's mess and apologizing in the same breath for the fact that they would not find it quite up to the standard of a naval wardroom. His gleaming smile flashed again and he added:

"I think we can provide English breakfasts of bacon and eggs — but only if we hurry before our barbarian cook can turn them into one of his wretched curries."

★ ★ ★

Despite Panjit Sangh's doubts the English-style breakfast was excellent, and when Mason bid good-bye to his flight companions an hour later he felt fit to tackle the job ahead. The aircrew, who had tactfully refrained from showing any direct interest into the unspecified nature of his mission, exchanged handshakes heartily but failed to keep the curiosity out of their eyes as he left the mess in the company of the young Indian.

"Intelligence bloke, I suppose," said the Flight Lieutenant after the door had closed. And then a sharp frown from his Captain made him return with a shrug to his coffee.

Outside the mess the jeep that had brought them across the airstrip was still waiting. The driver, a Sikh private wearing a turban and carrying a submachine-gun slung across his shoulder stiffened to attention as they approached.

Panjit Sangh smiled, almost apologetically, and said:

"I have been ordered to take you

straight to Colonel Samdar Rao, the Commanding Officer of the Tagantse sector. After that I will be free to take you to the prison compounds to talk to the Chinese we have captured — or anywhere else that you may wish to go."

"That's fine." Mason climbed into the back of the jeep and added. "I gather that it was Tagantse sector where our missing rifles have started to reappear?"

Sangh nodded. "Correct, Captain. The Tagantse area is one of the main attacking areas for the Chinese. The pass from Tibet provides one of the few routes along which they can transport their heavy field guns. The fighting, apart from the Walong area where the Chinese still threaten to break through towards the Brahmaputra river and the Assam plains, has been some of the heaviest along the whole frontier."

The young Lieutenant seated himself beside Mason in the back of the jeep and broke off the chain of his conversation to pass an unnecessarily crisp order to the driver. The jeep snarled into life and jolted forwards, accelerating fast, and then Sangh turned back to Mason.

"It is a matter of twenty-five miles to Colonel Rao's headquarters. The road is somewhat bumpy but providing this one-time mule driver does not run us over the edge of a gorge we should arrive in a little more than the hour."

Mason nodded as though satisfied and then transferred his gaze to watch one of the Air Force Dakotas that was rumbling into position for a take-off run along the single strip of broad concrete. The sound of its engines echoed clearly in the still mountain air and rose to a high-pitched whine as she began to gather speed. Mason glanced casually sideways as the plane began to lift and took the opportunity to study the man beside him.

Panjit Sangh was very young, probably in his early twenties. He was a bare inch shorter than Mason, and although slimmer his easy movements suggested a fluid strength. His dark eyes were as lively as his proud smile and his face was elegantly handsome. Mason distrusted the air of elegance, even though he had to wryly admit that the weakness to play the dandy was perhaps his own basic fault. The difference was that his own charm was reserved for women, and for the earned moments when he could relax. He could drop the elegance the moment the going became rough, but he wasn't sure that Panjit Sangh could do the same. Mason had the feeling that they could become formal enemies as easily as friends.

The Dakota was climbing high now and the momentary distraction was past. Mason's mind registered the final note that there was a long strip of sticking plaster behind Sangh's left ear and then the young Lieutenant had dropped his gaze from the plane in the sky.

Mason said calmly. "Have your people found any more of our weapons since the original report?"

Sangh shook his head. "None, Captain. The officers and N.C.O.s of all sectors along the front have been asked to keep their eyes open for any British weapons captured from Chinese prisoners. But all the reports have been negative."

"So all we have to go on are the three rifles that have turned up in this sector?"

"Correct. Two were found on captured prisoners. The third I took from a dead Chinese on the battlefield."

"You?" Mason was surprised. "I hadn't realized that you were the officer concerned."

Sangh smiled and lightly pressed two fingers to the strip of plaster behind his ear. "Yes, Captain. That was where I received this. A grenade explosion knocked me unconscious and separated me from my patrol. I collected the rifle on my way back to our lines. It is one reason why Colonel Rao assigned me as your aide. He said that as I had helped to start this thing I might as well help you to finish it. It was also a compromise between my desire to get back to the front, and the doctor's insistence that I wasn't really fit." He shrugged. "Perhaps it is as well. It keeps me from the fighting, but at least it is better than being sent back to the rear."

Mason grinned. "I'll try and get my

job done quickly so that you don't miss too much of the fun."

For once Panjit Sangh did not show his perfect teeth. He said seriously. "It is not fun, Captain. The Chinese must be stopped and India has need of all her officers."

Mason was silent for a moment, then he said.

"Do you think you can hold the Chinese back?"

"We must," the Indian said flatly. "Here on the frontier we are not only fighting for the defence of India but for the peace of the world. While we can restrict the conflict to a border war it cannot develop. But if the Chinese break through and begin a real invasion of India then world sympathy will become military aid. Active support for us will mean active support for the Chinese. From there it is not even a step to world war."

Mason nodded sombrely. "I can understand why you grudge your time."

Sangh suddenly smiled again. "Perhaps I over-estimate my own importance."

Mason grinned, and suddenly decided

that the Indian Lieutenant had no more faults than any other pride-flushed officer at the start of his career. And he was learning fast.

They were well clear of the airstrip now and were climbing along a twisted road that was not much more than a widened mule track above the plain. The terrain was rugged, steep slopes of gravel and shale, occasional dry bushes and carefully stacked cairns of stones to guide Buddhist pilgrims towards Tibet. A twist in the trail shut the plain from view and sheer rock walls formed a forbidding barrier ahead. Their engine made the only sound to violate the silence, and then Mason heard the faint crunch of distant artillery.

Sangh said: "We are still a long way behind the battle-front, but sound carries a long way in this thin air."

Mason nodded, and then heard another sound; a faint snarl.

"What's that?"

Sangh pointed ahead where the road curved in a vast loop across the side of the mountain before apparently vanishing through a solid rock-face. There a cloudy puff ball of dust almost blotted out a dinky toy replica of their own jeep.

"Over there," Sangh said. He spoke to his driver and leaned forward to take the leather binocular case that the man passed him from the front seat. He removed the high powered field glasses and held them to his eyes for a moment.

"Red Cross," he said at last. "I can't imagine what it is doing up there though. It didn't come from the airstrip."

Mason accepted the offered glasses and looked for himself. The jeep was sucked close by the strong lenses and he clearly made out the red cross on the white background.

"Three passengers," he observed. "Including the driver." He turned and returned the glasses to their owner. Panjit Sangh took another look and then gave an order to his driver. The man nodded and the jeep increased speed.

"They should not be heading into this area without an escort," Sangh explained. "I think we had better catch them."

Mason glanced down the steep slope to their left where a chain of boulders lay along the valley bottom far below. The edge of the slope was less than a yard from the jeep's nearside wheels as the vehicle accelerated but he refrained from comment. Instead he watched the second jeep high up on the loop of the road ahead.

Conversation lagged by mutual consent as they snarled in pursuit. Their vehicle was bumping and jolting so violently that conversation would have been difficult anyway. The Sikh driver handled the wheel confidently and despite the dizzy drop that awaited them Mason allowed himself to inwardly relax, realizing that Panjit Sangh had a tendency to belittle the competence of his men. They began to overhaul the distant jeep quite rapidly. The leading vehicle was in no apparent hurry and was motoring quite steadily around the bends.

The rock wall at the far end of the valley gradually separated to reveal a narrow pass as they swept around the mountain's flank. The far stretch of the road just before the lofty entrance was a series of ugly-looking S bends where it wound round ribs of bulging rock in the mountainside and here the first jeep slowed practically to a crawl as its driver inched his way with utmost care. The turbaned Sikh glanced back at Mason and his officer and flashed a quick grin that promised a fast end to the chase.

They reached the last half-mile of the zig-zag section and the Sikh showed his respect by easing his foot fractionally on the pedal and allowing the speedometer needle to drop to forty. The broad tyres shrieked and skidded as he slithered round the first bend and the jeep raced into the next one as his foot stamped down again. The great open void of the valley seemed to yaw before them, three thousand feet of empty space before the rocks of the valley bottom, and then the Sikh was braking again. They lurched round the first bulging rib of the mountain and headed for the next.

Panjit Sangh was grinning widely and almost reluctantly he spoke an order. The jeep slowed to a less suicidal speed.

Mason forced a tight smile.

"I can't say I'm sorry," he admitted.

Sangh showed his teeth ruefully.

"I like to go fast," he said. "But like wine and women it is the things that we like that can lead to our downfall. Besides, I think Colonel Rao would court martial my ghost if I allowed this muleteer to drive us both over the edge."

They were only a quarter-mile behind their quarry now, and they watched it vanish from sight through the lofty walls of the pass ahead. Their Sikh driver was taking the bends more carefully, but still with an easy confidence. Mason glanced at the stomach-fluttering drop on their left and decided that if anything it was becoming more sheer and even deeper, and was inwardly relieved that the young Indian beside him had the sense to curb his own and his driver's exuberance. If they had overshot one of the bends then the moment they left the road they would have been technically dead.

Then before he could fully adjust to the sense of reprieve there was an abrupt and fiercely echoing clatter of gunfire from the pass ahead.

Mason's mind was caught napping but even so his right hand dipped instinctively to snap open the stiff leather flap of the revolver holster at his hip. Panjit Sangh sat bolt upright, hesitant for a moment as he stared along the valley. Gunfire echoed again from the hidden pass and then the young Indian reached for his own revolver and snapped an order. He grinned wryly at Mason as the jeep leapt forward and said:

"This time I have an excuse — and my ghost must take its chances."

Mason nodded and drew his revolver, his muscles bunching with tension as they skidded along the dizzy edges of that hideous drop. The next few minutes were a nightmare of reckless driving, with one moment the solid rock wall of the mountain rushing towards them and the next aiming straight at the empty sky. The Sikh handled the wheel as though the devil himself was there to guide him, flinging the snarling jeep within inches of the point of no return and heaving it back to safety again until cold fear skewered through Mason's stomach and pinned him to his seat. Even Panjit Sangh, despite his professed taste for speed, was turning pale beneath his dark skin, but the sound of shooting still came from the pass and he with-held the order to slow down.

Dirt and stones showered away from their screeching tyres as their stiffly-braced driver heaved hard on the wheel to avoid a head-on crash into the mountain face, and then again they were pointing into the void before clearing the last of the bulging series of ribs. The Sikh pulled hard on the wheel again but this time the jeep continued to skid outwards in an uncontrollable, tyre-burning slide.

Mason saw the long fall to death coming up to meet them and flung himself desperately across the body of Panjit Sangh. In the same moment their driver also shifted his weight as far as possible on to the empty passenger seat beside him. The combined weight of all three men pressing down on the right side of the vehicle caused the jeep to tilt and the nearside wheels gripped again in the loose dirt. The offside wheels were spinning wildly through space as the jeep slewed round the projecting buttress of rock and then all four wheels were touching down again on solid earth.

The jeep wobbled crazily as the Sikh driver pulled himself back into position behind the wheel, and Mason could feel the sweat freezing along his spine as he struggled upright. They were on the straight now but there was no time for relief. The rearing rock walls that formed the mouth of the pass were already towering above them.

They shot through the opening with the roaring snarl of the jeep's straining engine reverberating like thunder through the narrow defile. Here the ground opened out again beyond the rock walls in a long shallow depression. The terrain was a jagged black sea of rocks and boulders except for the narrow ribbon of road that ran along the centre. And half-way along the ribbon lay the overturned wreck of the jeep they had followed up the valley. Approaching the wreck was a scattered party of Chinese soldiers who immediately began to scurry back into the protecting rocks as the army jeep appeared.

Most of the Chinese retreated backwards, facing their new enemy and firing desperately with their automatic weapons.

3

Command Headquarters

The Chinese were taken by surprise. The sound of the jeep they had ambushed, and then clatter of their own weapons, had drowned the sound of the army jeep until the moment that it came bursting into the narrow defile. Mason counted six soldiers and an officer, one soldier sprawling face down on the track, and three more bodies beside the overturned jeep. Then the Chinese opened fire as they scrambled back to cover.

Their turbaned driver had unslung his machine-gun from his shoulder as they roared through the straight into the pass, and now he held it clumsily while he drove with one hand. Mason loosed one impossible shot with his revolver as the lurching jeep swerved wildly to escape the first burst of Chinese fire, and then he grabbed the submachine-gun from the driver's hand.

Panjit Sangh was already pumping off shots from his own revolver as Mason stood upright in the back of the careering jeep. The Marine Captain hugged the machine-gun with the fervour of a starved lover embracing a woman, his feet wide apart to maintain his balance as he squeezed the trigger. The stream of tracer fire ripped through the air above their driver's head and sprayed in a murderous sweep across the width of the track. The Chinese officer who had stayed back to cover his men somersaulted backwards with flailing limbs as the bullets crashed into his body and the slowest of the retreating soldiers screamed as the scarlet holes punched into his spine.

In the same moment the jeep's windscreen disintegrated into a splintering star pattern of flying glass and the Sikh driver skidded the vehicle into a violent stop. Mason saw the bright red splash appear across the man's temple and then the force of the impact hurled him into the empty front seat. As he hit face down a blaze of fire screamed above him, searching the empty space where he had been standing only seconds ago.

Panjit Sangh had leapt from the moving jeep a split second before its jarring halt. He landed on one knee in a skidding crouch and with the heavy army revolver already blasting in his hand. The Chinese soldier who had fired the last burst at Mason gave a blubbering yell and dropped his gun, stumbling back into the rocks with one arm hanging uselessly.

The door of the jeep had crashed open and ignoring the carpet of broken glass across the front seat Mason wriggled in a fast slithering movement through the opening. He landed in the dirt on his elbows and knees with the machine-gun still clamped in his hands. Panjit Sangh was only a yard away, steadying himself on one knee with the smoking revolver still held at the ready. Apart from the three bodies on the track the Chinese had vanished.

There was an instant of silence and then the scrambling sound of nailed boots kicking on rocks as the remaining Chinese fled. Panjit Sangh was on his feet with a swift, straightening thrust of his legs, and his dark face wore an expression of fanatic joy as he plunged in pursuit. The revolver jumped and roared again in his hand and the bullet sang blindly through the wasteland of ugly black rocks. Sangh sprinted forward and vanished after the Chinese.

Mason, despite his less-dignified sprawling position, was only seconds behind him. The black rocks were a devil's maze, and the four Chinese had been completely swallowed. Panjit Sangh had paused to listen for any guiding sounds of flight and Mason caught him as he attempted to dive even deeper into the hopeless terrain.

"Hold it. Lieutenant!"

Mason had to make the words an order and forcibly restrain the young Indian. He went on breathlessly:

"You'll never catch them in this. And if you try they'll have all the advantages. They can just sit down in any crack or crevice and simply gun you as you go past. It's perfect country for ambushing any pursuit."

Sangh hesitated, his eyes moving from the firm hand on his shoulder to meet Mason's sharp blue eyes. Then the fire in him lost heat and his smile showed faintly.

"Of course, Captain. I should have realized."

His body relaxed reluctantly and he glanced again at Mason's hand on his shoulder. Mason smiled and took the hand away. There was no sound now that the echoes of Sangh's last shot had died away and they turned and made their way back to the road.

Their Sikh driver was waiting for them by the jeep. The man looked very unsteady and was dabbing at his temple with a grubby rag to keep the blood from spilling into his eyes. He had picked up Mason's revolver, but whether from the instinct of self-defence or with the intentions of supporting his officers was hard to tell. Panjit Sangh hurried towards the man, but Mason kept his submachine-gun levelled and cautiously inspected the dead Chinese.

The officer lay grotesquely, almost

obscenely, on his back with his arms and legs flung wide. He was a Lieutenant and his agonized face was very young, not much more than a boy. Mason's jaw tightened and he turned away. The soldier he had shot was equally rigid in death and it was only the third man of whom he was wary; the soldier who had already been lying face-down on the track when they arrived. After a moment he was satisfied that the third man was also harmless; he had been shot in the head.

He turned back to Panjit Sangh who was inspecting the cut on their driver's temple.

"How is he, Lieutenant?"

"He will live," Sangh said cheerfully. "The cut is deep and messy but he comes from a hardy race. The broken glass must have hit him when the windscreen smashed. Perhaps our friends from the Red Cross will have a first aid kit with which to patch him up."

Mason nodded and all three moved towards the overturned jeep farther down the track. The vehicle lay on one side and all three of its occupants had been thrown out. Two of the bodies appeared to be lying where they had fallen while the third had apparently attempted to put up some kind of defence. He was an Indian private in army uniform, and he slumped against the back of the jeep with a rifle lying close to his trailing fingers. Mason made a quick mental reconstruction and guessed that the private had been responsible for killing the third Chinese before the main party had cut him down.

He moved closer to the last two bodies and then stared. One of them was a woman. She wore faded green dungarees, similar to those of the man beside her, but now the outline of the breasts was evident. One glance was enough to show that the man was dead. His position on the ground indicated that he was probably the jeep's driver and there were vivid red stains across his back. Mason lowered his gun and knelt by the woman.

There was a plum-sized bruise above her left eye but she was still breathing faintly. Her glossy, jet-black hair was secured by a neat white band above her temples but now the smooth waves lay in disorder around her head. The face was thinly beautiful and her skin was the dark gold of mixed blood.

Panjit Sangh noticed Mason's interest. "Is she alive?"

Mason nodded. "She's just unconscious, must have given her head a terrific clout on something when the jeep went over."

The Indian Lieutenant forgot about their driver and came closer.

"I should have guessed," he said. "The red cross should have told me."

Mason looked up, and then understood. "You know her?"

"Yes, Captain. Doctor Karen Langford. Her work covers the whole of this area, and despite the fact that there is a war taking place she insists upon dodging about from village to village to attend to her practice. As she would not leave the army provided her with the Red Cross vehicle to replace her own, in the hope that it would mean something to the Chinese if they succeeded in pushing forward the front line and she were to fall into their hands." He shrugged wryly. "Now it appears that the Chinese

42

do not respect the sign of the red cross anyway."

Mason grimaced. "What the hell was that patrol doing here? I thought we were still miles from the firing line."

Sangh grinned. "We are not all that far away. Perhaps ten miles. The road runs in an approximate parallel to the front before swinging in to Tagantse." His face became serious and he added: "But I also would like to know what they were doing. It was only a small scouting patrol so perhaps they were attempting to survey the airstrip we have just left. They may have reasoned that the doctor's jeep had just come from the strip and that its occupants, if captured, could provide them with the information they needed. Although it seems to have been a clumsy attempt, and they soon took fright when we arrived."

Mason was examining the unconscious woman for any other sign of injury and said calmly. "They were in enemy territory and no doubt they believed that we had more reinforcements coming when they fled. The whole ambush must have been badly arranged, but their officer was no more than a boy and obviously inexperienced."

Panjit Sangh stiffened slightly. Then he said coldly:

"I will find the doctor's medical kit."

Mason looked up as the Indian Lieutenant turned away, and then he realized where he had been tactless. The reference to the Chinese officer's youth had been taken as an affront by the Indian who could not have been many years older. Mason smiled inwardly and made a mental note to be more careful in future.

Panjit Sangh found the medical kit and opened it on the ground. He left Mason to attend to the woman and turned back to their driver who stood patiently beside them, the only sign of discomfort the quick blinking of his eyes as the blood threatened to blind him. The Indian Lieutenant's treatment was somewhat brusque, but the hardy Sikh bore it stolidly. Mason concentrated on reviving the doctor.

He found a bottle of smelling salts

and after supporting her shoulders against one knee and his arm he moved the bottle slowly beneath her nostrils. She stirred and her face wrinkled distastefully as she pulled her head away. Mason held the bottle close again and her eyes flickered open.

"Don't panic," he said calmly. "The cavalry has arrived and the Chinese have gone."

The olive-coloured eyes searched his face with a wide stare but her face registered no emotion. Then she attempted to move her head but Mason dropped the salts bottle and held her still, gently but firmly gripping the lower part of her face.

"Don't look round," he said. He waited a moment before the sick look in her eyes showed that she had understood, and then broke the news softly. "Both of your friends are dead."

"Hakim — " She spoke the name wretchedly, fearfully.

"Both of them," Mason repeated. "I'm sorry."

She closed her eyes and squeezed

them hard for a moment. Then she opened them again and her hand pulled weakly at his wrist where he gripped her chin.

"It is all right." She had to steel herself. "I have seen death before. I will not panic."

Mason nodded and helped her to her feet. She stood against him trembling, and after she had prepared herself she looked around her. She swallowed hard as she saw her driver.

"Poor Hakim, he was just an orderly. He knew only a little of medicine, and nothing of war." She pulled her eyes away. "And the soldier too. We should never have given him a ride."

She turned to face Panjit Sangh who was still endeavouring to fix a dressing to the Sikh's forehead, and then moved unsteadily away from Mason's supporting arm.

"Please," she said. "That — that is my job. I will finish it."

Sangh hesitated, and then the perfect smile appeared.

"It is all right. I can manage."

"Please," she persisted. "I am a doctor."

Mason caught Sangh's eye as he opened his mouth to argue and the Indian understood. He smiled more gallantly than before and allowed her to take over the task of attending to the Sikh.

By the time that the dressing was properly fixed the familiar movements had helped to steady the doctor considerably. While she worked Mason and Panjit Sangh carefully removed the bodies of her companions from the road and laid them in the shadow of the wrecked jeep. The Indian Lieutenant then brought their own jeep up and manœuvred it through the gap. Mason kept an alert eye open for any possible return of the Chinese, even though he was practically certain that by now the remains of the scouting patrol would be half-way back to their own lines.

Karen Langford gave the Sikh a faint smile as she finished her doctoring, and then she knelt to re-pack her medical kit. She was still shaken but now there was curiosity in her eyes as she glanced up at Mason.

"You are a British officer. Does that mean that the British are sending troops to help fight the Chinese?"

Mason smiled. "I'm afraid not." He rolled out the stock cover phrase for any mission that meant contact with a foreign army. "I'm the only one. I'm here in an advisory capacity."

"I see." She sounded as though she saw only too well and recognized a rebuke. Then she attempted to cover up and said weakly: "I suppose I should thank you for coming to my rescue."

He tried to mend the breach with his smile. "Don't forget Lieutenant Sangh. He did equally as much. And he was all set to chase them all the way back to China."

Sangh rejoined them.

"Captain Mason is too modest," he said. "But it is time that we continued on our way. When we reach Tagantse I will see to it that a burial patrol is sent out to attend to these bodies."

They returned to the jeep and this time

the doctor was seated beside Mason in the back. There was a momentary protest from the Sikh when Panjit Sangh took the wheel, but after a crisp order from his officer the man reluctantly relinquished his duty. The jeep's engine roared into full life and after a minute the battleground was lost from view behind the black rocks.

* * *

Thirty-five minutes later they arrived at the front line command post at Tagantse. They were stopped twice by Indian Army patrols as they entered the village, but were waved on almost immediately as Panjit Sangh identified himself. On the far side of the village was a handful of partially isolated buildings that the Indian Army had commandeered for its forward headquarters, and here some prefabricated wooden huts had been hastily thrown into position. One hut had been painted with a scarcely-dry red cross to house the Medical Officer and here they left Karen Langford and their wounded driver.

An armed corporal moved to bar their way as they finally braked to a stop outside the largest commandeered building and a sergeant came running. There was a brief exchange of words that Mason could not follow and then the corporal backed away and Panjit Sangh indicated with a fluid gesture that they were to go with the sergeant. They both swung down from the jeep and followed the man into the building, a large converted farmhouse that was an ant heap of hurrying officers and non-coms. Everybody seemed to be talking at once and typewriters clattered as though only a continuous thousand words per minute could possibly win the war.

They were handed over to another sergeant and then had to wait for almost twenty minutes before they could get into the inner sanctum that was the main command room. Here it was quieter and more orderly, although the racket still penetrated from outside. Vast maps adorned the walls and bore the concentrated scrutiny of a small group of staff officers, two Majors and a Captain. A second Captain was arguing into a telephone and behind the large desk sat a small, dapper grey-haired man in the uniform of a Colonel. The Colonel rose almost wearily to his feet.

"So you are Captain Mason. I hear that you had an interesting trip up from the airstrip." He extended a hand across his desk and added: "I am Colonel Samdar Rao, and I have the misfortune to be in command of this mad-house."

They shook hands briefly and then the Colonel sank back into his chair and demanded Panjit Sangh's report. The young Lieutenant gave a concise account of the ambush in the pass and added his belief that the Chinese had been reconnoitring the airstrip.

Samdar Rao frowned. "Did they stumble upon Doctor Langford by chance, or was it a deliberate attempt to take prisoners?"

"I think the latter. The doctor told us as we drove here that they saw nothing of the Chinese until the attack actually began, the patrol was hiding in the rocks. Her driver and orderly, a man named

Hakim was killed, and so was a private of the fourth division named Rahman. The private had approached her in Jangi village near the airstrip where she had attended a patient and asked her for a ride back here to Tagantse. It seems he became separated from his unit when they were moved up to the front yesterday evening."

Samdar Rao nodded. "All right, Lieutenant Sangh, we'll be prepared for a Chinese strike towards the airstrip." He turned to face Mason and smiled sadly.

"Forgive me, Captain, if I prove an awkward host. But attempting to organize a war in these crazy hills draws heavily on my time."

Mason smiled. "I understand. Even to me my mission seems of minor importance now that I am here on the scene."

The Colonel nodded again, his head jerking stiffly. "Have you any idea of how the Chinese have obtained British weapons?" he asked.

Mason explained the three daring raids on the two British naval bases and finished: "The rifles that appeared here are so far the only clue we have. Two teams of investigators are still combing Singapore and Hong Kong, but they're turning in only negative reports. I'm hoping to get a lead from this end."

"I confess I cannot understand it." This time Samdar Rao's head jerked from side to side instead of up and down. Then he looked up. "But that is one problem which I shall be happy to leave entirely upon your shoulders, Captain. You have Lieutenant Sangh to assist you, and — " He drew an official-looking pass from his desk and wrote rapidly, flourishing his signature at the bottom. "This will permit you entry into the prison compound on the other side of Tagantse. It is only a transit camp from which the prisoners are shipped farther back behind the lines when opportunity permits, but the two Chinese who were found bearing your missing rifles have been retained."

Mason accepted the pass, and with it recognized his dismissal. He saluted smartly and Panjit Sangh followed his example. Samdar Rao wished them luck and then turned back to the more serious business of arranging extra protection for the threatened airstrip.

Mason and Sangh returned to their jeep and in the same moment they heard the violent orchestra of artillery crashing out somewhere to the north. Sangh stared towards the distant rumblings for a moment, his dark face grim yet regretful, then he turned to Mason and smiled wryly.

"Let us go and beat some answers out of these damned Chinks," he said. "Before the front line starts to do the Victor Silvester two-step up and down the hillsides. It changes with every battle."

4

Bloodstains on a White Flag

THE prison compound was situated half a mile from the village and was simply a large barbed wire cage strung on ten-foot high concrete posts. The top two feet of the wire slanted inwards and the top strand was doubly barbed with vicious, glinting needles that made it impossible for a hand to grip the wire between them. The cage was forty foot square and contained almost half a hundred dejected Chinese in grubby uniforms of the Red Army. It was guarded by a detachment of Indian troops under the command of a Sergeant.

Panjit Sangh stopped the jeep, for he had not wasted time in attempting to find another driver, and together he and Mason approached the cage. The Sergeant looked curiously up and down Mason's Marine uniform but restrained from comment. He glanced at the pass they had received from Samdar Rao and after a moment of parley with Panjit Sangh led the way to the single gateway to the compound. He bellowed an order as the gate was opened up and two of his men moved briskly to accompany them, unslinging their submachine-guns in readiness. All five passed through the barbed wire gate and then the guards re-locked it behind them.

Most of the prisoners were standing upright, their sallow faces sullen and hateful. They had all been issued with blankets which draped over their misery-shrunken shoulders, but they all appeared to be in reasonably good health. Some lay huddled in their blankets on the ground, but all stared hard at the new arrivals with tense, nervous eyes.

"Conditions are bad and they have no roof, but they have blankets and are allowed to build fires at night," Panjit Sangh explained. "We will move them into a properly constructed camp as soon as possible."

Mason nodded but said nothing. He

sensed that even though the present conditions were unavoidable, Panjit Sangh would not be personally troubled if they remained unchanged. The Indian's face said more than his words. He hated the Chinese, and considering the unprovoked attack on his country he had good cause.

A Chinese officer moved away from the rest of the prisoners and came to meet them, standing stiffly to attention and making a formal salute.

Panjit Sangh smiled sardonically and made a casual answering gesture that was a deliberate insult.

"This is our prize," he said. "Lieutenant Cheng Wu. He is the only officer we have captured since the last batch of prisoners was transferred, but that is only because so few of them dare accompany their men to the front."

The Chinese Lieutenant's eyes wished murder. He glared for a moment and then switched his gaze abruptly to Mason.

"So India has screamed to her capitalist friends for help," he said in a tightly controlled voice. "It will make no difference. Nothing can withstand the might of the People's Republic of China." He looked back at Sangh. "But what do you want?"

"We want to speak to two of your soldiers. A man called Feng Tung and a man called Su Yat," said Sangh crisply.

"On what grounds?"

Sangh grinned and pointed at his feet. "On this ground here. Now bring them."

"These men have already stated their names, ranks and numbers," the Chinese recited tartly. "The Geneva convention says — "

"You have as much respect for the Geneva convention as I have for your Chinese backside," Sangh cut in bluntly. "Now order those men to step forward."

Cheng Wu bristled. "I protest!"

"So," Sangh shrugged. "Now you have protested."

The Chinese went slightly pale around the lips in an effort to compress his temper. Then he turned on his heel and shouted an order. For a moment there was no response, and then two of the prisoners shuffled forward, hugging their blankets about them as though the

can dispense with Lieutenant Cheng. We'll take the two soldiers outside the compound and the Sergeant can interrogate them there."

"I must protest," Cheng snapped. "If my soldiers are to be interrogated then it must be in my presence. There must be no filthy capitalist torture. The Geneva convention says — "

"Shut your barbarian mouth," Panjit Sangh said brusquely. He turned to give orders to the Sergeant and immediately one of the armed guards pushed Cheng back with an unrespecting prod of his submachine-gun. The second guard and the Sergeant began to shepherd the two frightened soldiers towards the gateway.

Cheng Wu still protested angrily, ignoring a reassurance from Mason that no torture methods would be used against his men. Finally the Chinese began screaming insults and Mason turned away.

The two Chinese soldiers were taken to a wooden guard hut fifty yards away from the compound and the door was firmly closed to shut out the last of Lieutenant

Cheng's shouted protests. Two chairs were pulled into the centre of the room and the prisoners were seated with Mason, Sangh and the Sergeant ranged around them in a half circle. The two guards stood with their backs to the door and their weapons levelled. The unfortunate Chinese stared from face to face with terrified eyes.

The questioning began and it was soon apparent that the Indian Sergeant's ability to communicate with the prisoners was limited. Besides which it was clear that Cheng's last shouted orders still over-rode their fear of their captors. The two Chinese maintained a wincing silence. After two hours Mason felt a growing desire to grip the two blank yellow faces and bang the backs of their heads together.

Panjit Sangh sensed Mason's exasperation. He smiled meaningly and said: "You grow weary, Captain. May I suggest that you return to the jeep for half an hour while the Sergeant and I continue the interrogation. I am sure that alone we can produce some results."

Mason could guess at the methods that would be used while his back was turned, and he was almost tempted. Then he said: "No, Lieutenant. No rough treatment. We'll give it another half-hour and then try again tomorrow. We'll lock them up separately where Lieutenant Cheng can't get at them and see whether a night of solitary confinement can loosen their tongues."

Panjit Sangh nodded reluctantly and then he and the Sergeant redoubled their efforts. Mason watched, and although he had forbidden actual violence he sensed from the faces of the prisoners that the two Indians were making some pretty bloodthirsty threats. However, when he voiced his suspicions Panjit Sangh merely looked pained and made a bland denial. At the end of the half-hour they had made no progress and Mason insisted that the Chinese be locked away in solitary to think things over.

He drove back to Tagantse beside the slightly ruffled Panjit Sangh and did some quiet thinking of his own. He was convinced that the two soldiers were merely keeping silent on Cheng's orders, and that Cheng was simply refusing to cooperate on principle. And he had a strangely unsettling feeling that even if he did learn where the two Chinese had *found* their British weapons, he would still be no closer to the answers he had been sent to find.

* * *

That night Mason dined in the long wooden hut that served as the officers' mess, having spent the afternoon in installing himself in an empty ground floor room of one of the commandeered buildings near Command Headquarters that had been allotted as his billet. Throughout the day heavy troop movements had been hurrying to and fro through Tagantse and the battle sounds had continued their crash and roar to the north. Now the noise and activity had abated and although an occasional convoy still rumbled through the dirt streets of the village there was a minimum of artillery explosions from the front.

Samdar Rao was still detained in his control room, but several of his staff officers were seated around the long table. They ate hurriedly and talked briefly, mentioning only out of politeness that the day's fighting had caused no changes along the disputed border line. No ground had been either won or lost. An elderly Major added bitterly that the only loss on both sides had been in lives. Directly opposite Mason Karen Langford ate and listened in silence. She had acknowledged Mason as he entered, but had said little since. Now he studied her curiously from time to time as the meagre scraps of talk fluttered about them.

The large bruise on her forehead had not been covered and now it looked plum-coloured as well as plum-sized. She still wore her faded green overall, sensible wear for visiting remote mountain villages, but it failed to hide her slender femininity. Her thin, dark gold face bore a faint expression of anger and she kept her eyes downcast towards her plate. Mason was both attracted and intrigued.

The two officers on either side of her rose to leave, making almost sincere apologies as they hurried back towards Command Headquarters. Apart from Panjit Sangh on Mason's right there were only three officers left at the far end of the table and they were concentrating solely on their food, and Mason judged it time to ask after the Doctor's health.

She looked up and smiled faintly.

"It is not too bad, thank you. My head still aches, but your camp Medical Officer insisted that I took a sedative and rested for this afternoon. It was he who invited me here as his guest, but he has been called away to attend to some casualties from the front." Her face darkened. "They bring them in every day. Dozens of them. It is so senseless."

"You are not an Army Doctor?"

She shook her head. "My practice is in the villages. I have my clinic here in Tagantse and it is bad fortune that the Army must choose this village for their headquarters. It is bad for the villagers and I shall be glad when it is over."

Mason recognized the note of reproof

and said: "You sound as though you blame the Indian Army — why not the Chinese?"

She looked up sharply, searching for a hidden meaning. His blue eyes held none and after a moment she smiled faintly.

"I do not blame them. But sometimes I can be angry with them. They treat war as all-important, almost to enjoy it. To them the civilian population is a nuisance that gets in their way. They have no time for the tragedy that faces my people, perhaps that is not their fault, but I resent it."

Panjit Sangh watched her curiously as she talked. The young Lieutenant had either forgiven or forgotten the fact that he had been over-ruled at the prison compound and had soon regained his elegant cheerfulness. Now he was looking serious again and spoke before Mason could frame an answer.

"But surely you see that the war *is* all-important. The Chinese must be held back. The handful of hill villagers you worry about are so inconsequential in the face of the threat to the whole of India."

Karen Langford gave him a hostile glance. She said bitingly: "If war and conquest are the only things of importance then you are no better than the Chinese. It is people who matter."

"What Lieutenant Sangh means," Mason interrupted tactfully, "is that the rest of India is also made up of countless simple and innocent villages like those in your care. And that the failure to check the Chinese advance here on the frontier will mean that the suffering you have witnessed will be multiplied all over the sub-continent. Stopping that spread of suffering is the importance of the war."

Panjit Sangh looked at him uncertainly, not sure whether in fact his meaning had been correctly interpreted, while the Doctor looked slightly mollified. I should have gone into politics, Mason thought, not intelligence, and then the door opened and he was relieved by the entry of Colonel Samdar Rao and two of his officers.

There was a quick scraping of chairs as the Commanding Officer appeared but the formalities were brief. Samdar

Rao took the vacant chair beside the Doctor and the officers, both Majors, sat on either side of them. The Colonel was looking very tired and strained but he greeted the gathering cordially and with a special word for the Doctor. An orderly was already standing to attention to receive the new orders.

As he waited for his meal to arrive Samdar Rao glanced across the table at Mason and remarked.

"I hope that you have finished the interrogation of the Chinese prisoners, Captain Mason. Because tomorrow may be too late. I'm sending most of them back."

At the word interrogation Karen Langford gave Mason a sharp look but he could not answer it. Instead he had to keep his face blank as he replied to the dapper little Colonel.

"The only two in which I have any interest are being confined separately. I hope that by morning they will be willing to talk."

Samdar Rao's head nodded, a gesture that could either be habit or approval.

"Then they can be retained. The Chinese have so many thousands of soldiers that I doubt if they will miss two." He smiled and then explained. "Tomorrow I am arranging an exchange of prisoners. Those in our compound here in return for an equal number of our own men captured by the Chinese in a battle two days ago."

Mason smiled his congratulations. "That's a good sign."

The Colonel nodded again. "The only one so far. The fighting has been heavy along this sector again today, and another savage battle has taken place in the Walong area where we are having difficulty in preventing a break-through. But if this exchange is successful it could lead to more negotiations, and possibly to an eventual cease-fire."

The Colonel continued to enthuse about the possibilities of his move, and Mason realized that his hopes were almost desperate. Samdar Rao badly wanted a sign of sanity from his ruthless enemies. Mason listened but kept his faint misgivings to himself. He felt that it was too early for the steam-rolling Chinese Army to make concessions and vaguely sensed that the Indian Commander was heading for disappointment.

After a few moments the waiter arrived with steaming plates and Karen Langford chose that moment to take her leave. Mason guessed that the Indian officers had little time to gossip and tactfully excused himself in order to accompany her. Samdar Rao who appeared to have little time for military protocol in his present surroundings, dismissed him with a brief nod, but as Mason left he saw a dark flicker of anger cross the face of Panjit Sangh. It took him a moment to recognize jealousy and he rebuked himself inwardly. It was unexpected, but intelligence should have taught him to anticipate the unexpected.

Outside the mess hut he took the Doctor's arm and sensed a slight withdrawal in her attitude. He said calmly.

"I felt that someone should see you safely back to your clinic. I hope you don't mind."

"I should have been safe," she said. But she allowed him to walk with her and did not pull her arm away. She held her head high and gazed up at the night sky with its sharp stars and bright moonlight. After a hundred yards of silence she voiced the thought that worried her.

"What did Colonel Rao mean when he referred to your interrogation of prisoners?"

Mason groaned inwardly but managed an exterior smile.

"Nothing much. I had to ask a few questions."

"And did you have to confine them to solitary imprisonment?"

"It won't hurt them." He tried to sound sincere. "I don't want their officer inciting them to resistance."

She said bitterly. "And this is in your advisory capacity!"

Mason wondered whether it was worth the effort to explain, but she quickened her pace and he decided against it. Before he could introduce a fresh topic of conversation they reached a stoutly constructed wooden building and he realized that this was her clinic. She removed her arm from his hand and half turned on the doorstep to face him.

"Good night, Captain — Captain Mason isn't it?"

He smiled, the debonair smile that was calculated to attract.

"It's Paul," he said. "Captain Mason sounds too pompous."

She opened the door and said stiffly. "Good night, *Captain Mason*." And then she stepped into darkness and closed the door behind her.

Mason smiled ruefully at the closed door.

"Good night, Doctor Langford," he said quietly. And then he walked thoughtfully back to his billet.

* * *

He was roughly awakened the next morning by an urgent hand shaking his shoulder and was half-way to his feet as his eyes opened and he recognized the anxious face of Panjit Sangh. The young Lieutenant's tunic was unbuttoned and he had obviously come straight from his own bed.

"Trouble, Captain," he said crisply. "Colonel Rao wants us both to report to him at once."

Mason didn't waste time with questions but scrambled straight into his uniform. He was still buckling on his revolver as he followed Sangh outside into the sharp morning air. An armed soldier awaited them and escorted them swiftly towards the Command Headquarters where two truck loads of troops were waiting to move off. Samdar Rao stood by the lead truck with a tall Major, one of the officers who had shared his table the night before. Both men looked grim and the dapper Colonel was controlling an obvious outburst of fury. In his hand he held a square of white cloth that was soiled with dark stains. He held it out as Mason and Sangh ran up and Mason recognized the stains as blood.

The Colonel said bitterly. "Captain Mason, I have bad news. I told you last night about my efforts to enact an exchange of prisoners. This morning

Major Radhaven led a small patrol to discuss terms with the Chinese in a section of no-man's-land in the hills. Both parties were to approach under a white truce flag." His fists tightened on the bloody rag in his hands. "This was the Chinese flag, Captain Mason. They had been butchered. But not by my troops — by civilians. The Major arrived in time to frighten off a large party of hill men who must have come from one of the mountain villages."

Samdar Rao paused and drew a deep breath. "Shots were exchanged, Captain Mason. Shots from modern rifles. Those illiterate hill men were armed with modern weapons."

Mason knew now why the Colonel had sent for him but waited for the dapper little Indian to finish.

"Captain Mason, Major Radhaven is now taking a larger patrol into the hills to search the surrounding villages and locate the murderers who ambushed the Chinese truce party. I want to know who organized those men and who supplied them with arms. And as the only illicit arms that have appeared on the frontier are those which you British have lost you and Lieutenant Sangh will accompany the Major on his mission."

Samdar Rao threw the bloodstained square of white savagely to the ground and walked bitterly away, leaving his crushed hopes in the dirt with the crumpled symbol.

5

The Man with the Shaven Head

Mason and Panjit Sangh rode with the tall Major Radhaven in the Major's jeep while the two lorries lumbered in their wake. The Major was a tight-lipped man with a straight, pencil-line moustache. His eyebrows were equally straight and narrow and his nose was thin. The whole face could have been caricatured in sharp lines with a minimum of curves. As they drove into the hills he explained more fully how he had found the Chinese truce party. He had heard the sound of the ambush but by the time he had rushed his own patrol to the spot the Chinese had been cut to pieces. They had been caught in a narrow ravine that was a perfect spot for their attackers. The Indian troops had opened fire to drive the hill men off and the ambushers had fled. Not a single Chinese had remained alive around their pathetic flag. The Major's account was given grimly, but he was not as emotional as his Colonel, and Mason summed him up as a better field officer than a staff man.

The road they followed was again little more than a widened mule track that twisted cruelly through the hills. The lorries struggled along it with frequent wheel-spinning halts that forced the troops inside to dismount and push them free, but within half an hour they reached the first village. The Major dismounted from his jeep and interrogated the villainous-looking headman while the troops, under a massive Sikh Sergeant, searched the houses. Nothing was found and they drove on to the next village in the area where they again drew a blank.

"It must be Ladrung," said Radhaven as he settled himself in the jeep and gave the driver the order to move off for the third time. He twisted in his seat to face Mason and Sangh and explained: "The ambushers fled in this direction and the village of Ladrung is the only one left within easy reach."

The mule-track road began to climb again, twisting higher into the mountains. It was also leading them back towards the battlefront and the continuous booming of artillery fire carried more clearly to their ears. The sound caused the sharp-faced Major's lips to tighten even more and he increased the pace of his little convoy.

After another four miles they reached the village of Ladrung, a score of crude, stone-built houses in a shallow depression that was skirted by the road. The houses were flat-roofed, most of them covered with dung laid out to dry for fuel. There were a few earth-walled stables housing mules, and dogs and chickens rooted among the poor vegetable patches. The villagers came out slowly as the convoy stopped and the troops dismounted, and Mason sensed instinctively that Radhaven had been right and that this was the village they wanted. The men were wild and unclean, and the signs of defiance were already there in their dark, angry faces.

The Indian Major got out of the jeep

and this time Mason got down beside him. The Marine Captain scented trouble and knew the value of a united front. Panjit Sangh ranged himself upon the Major's other flank.

Radhaven shouted orders and the big Sikh Sergeant was prompt to carry them out. The village headman was identified and brought before the three officers while the troops dispersed in units of four to search the buildings. The women of the village backed away but the men stood their ground sullenly and forced the soldiers to walk round them.

Radhaven pursed his lips and stared at the headman, a burly villain wearing baggy trousers and a crude sheepskin jacket that left his arms bare. The man's skin was black with dirt and his beard straggled. He stood with his arms dangling at his sides and his feet braced apart, his chin low and his eyes glowering upwards through heavy brows.

Radhaven said distastefully. "Sergeant Marijani, ask him his name."

The big Sikh, who dwarfed even this hefty villager, complied in a voice that snapped authority. The headman answered surlily. His name was Tarong.

"Ask him about the ambush this morning."

The big Sikh translated the question into the local dialect and there was a brief argument with the headman shaking his head and becoming flatly antagonistic. At last Marijani turned back to Radhaven, his face frankly contemptuous beneath his turban and magnificent black beard.

"He insists that he knows nothing, Major. But I do not believe him."

There was a moment of silence as the hill-man faced them stubbornly, and then an abrupt disturbance from the back of the village. There was a man's angry cry and the quick sound of a brief scuffle, followed by the shrill, frightened yelp of a woman. The searching soldiers converged on the spot in a rush of heavy boots, and then after another ever briefer scuffle a corporal appeared with his arms wrapped around half a dozen brand new automatic rifles. Behind him a group of his companions were holding back the most violent of the villagers. Marijani, who had automatically headed for the scene, now stopped and waited for his man to approach, his fiery eyes fixed accusingly on the headman.

"I found these in a cave at the back of the village," the corporal reported, using English for Mason's benefit. "There is a small arsenal there, sir. They were hidden beneath some sacks of grain."

Marijani took one of the rifles and shook it vigorously in the headman's face. Tarong flinched away but his mouth remained tightly closed and he refused to answer the Sergeant's demanding scorn. Mason looked past them and saw three more Indian soldiers reappearing from between the stone walls of the buildings, all with their arms laden with guns.

The Marine Captain examined the weapons one at a time, checking the serial numbers and then stacking them in a heap beside the Major's jeep. Radhaven and Panjit Sangh watched him as the now silent Marijani kept his severe gaze on the nervous Tarong. Mason counted sixteen brand new rifles and then glanced up at the corporal who affirmed that that was the lot. Then he looked at the two Indian officers.

"They're all ours," he said. "They're part of the haul that was stolen from the naval base in Singapore. The three rifles that have turned up in the hands of the Chinese were part of the same haul."

Panjit Sangh said slowly. "But did the Chinese take their rifles from the villagers, or did the villagers receive their rifles from the Chinese?"

Mason frowned. "I can't imagine the Chinese arming their enemies, so it seems that the original three weapons must have fallen into their hands by accident." He looked at Panjit Sangh. "The rifle that you found, Lieutenant, you took from a dead man on the battlefield. It's possible that he and the two Chinese prisoners found the weapons in the same way. If you remember, the man Feng Tung did admit that he had *found* his rifle before that damned Lieutenant Cheng chipped in to stop him telling us where."

Radhaven summed up. "So you think that all the rifles arrived through these people. But who is supplying them with the arms — and why?"

Mason said grimly. "Let's find out. If the headman won't talk maybe some of the others will."

Radhaven nodded and turned to the big Sikh.

"Organize the villagers into a line, Sergeant, and question the lot. And try and impress upon them that we're all allies against the Chinese. It might break down some of this resistance."

Marijani saluted smartly and began bellowing orders. The headman watched without comment as the rest of the villagers were formed into line by the efficient Indian troops, and then the corporal held him to one side as Mason accompanied the two Indian officers and Marijani along the line. The men were sullen and unresponsive to both threats and pleas and kept their mouths tightly shut. They could deny nothing and so they stayed silent. The interrogation had progressed half way along the short line when the sound of an approaching engine neared the village.

Marijani paused in his threatening

demands and for a moment all attention was distracted towards the sound. The engine increased in volume and then the square bonnet of a jeep struggled round a climbing bend in the mule-track road. The vehicle roared towards them and then braked sharply behind the tail-end of the last lorry. The driver was alone and Mason recognized the slim figure and glossy black hair as she shut off the engine and climbed down on to the road. She came towards them slowly, her olive-coloured eyes moving along the scowling faces of the villagers.

She stopped in front of them, her face angry. For a moment she looked at Mason and then she addressed her demand to Radhaven.

"What on earth is going on here? What are you doing?"

Mason cut in before the Major could answer.

"What is more to the point is what are you doing here?"

"I am a doctor." She looked at him curtly. "And I have a patient here. One of the women is expecting a baby." Her tone became sarcastic. "Perhaps the baby should be told to stay where it is because there is a war on."

"I'm sorry," Mason apologized. "I should have realized."

"Yes — you should. But what does this mean? Are you still in your *advisory capacity*?"

"Doctor Langford," Radhaven interrupted. "Captain Mason is here on a mission for his own country to trace some missing arms. These arms — " He pointed stiffly to the mound of rifles stacked against his jeep. "Someone has been supplying these villagers with the stolen weapons."

Karen Langford stared at him in amazement. "But these are simple village men. What would they want with arms? Who would want to supply them?"

"That is what we intend to find out." Redhaven went on to give a brief account of the way in which the Chinese truce party had been ambushed, and then finished: "You must understand that this is a serious matter."

"But I don't understand." The Doctor

was perplexed. "These are only simple mountain men. They know nothing of war."

Radhaven was becoming impatient, and he was not a ladies' man. He said bluntly: "Doctor Langford, we do not expect you to understand. We do not understand ourselves. Now please attend to your patient and kindly allow us to continue."

Hot blood flushed the dark gold skin of the Eurasian face, and for a moment Mason thought that she was about to make some violent outburst. Instead her mouth trembled for a moment and then she spun round and stalked swiftly away, disappearing between two of the rough-walled houses.

Radhaven turned immediately back to the villagers and nodded to Marijani to continue. Mason listened to the questioning without being able to understand the dialect, but the negative expressions showed that Marijani was making no headway. Mason's jaw tightened, and after a moment he excused himself from the party and followed the direction taken by the doctor. Radhaven simply nodded an uninterested dismissal but Panjit Sangh watched him out of sight.

He found the Doctor talking to one of the village women on the threshold of one of the drab stone houses. The village woman, an old crone in black rags, saw him approach and darted back inside the building. The Doctor turned angrily to face him.

"Doctor Langford," Mason smiled placatingly. "Can't you see that it's for their own good that we have to make these people talk. We must know who is trying to organize them and why."

"Then go back to your interrogation." She spoke the last word as though it tasted unclean.

Mason shrugged. "I'm afraid it isn't getting us very far. The men refuse to talk. For some reason they seem to consider us their enemies as much as the Chinese." He paused, and then suggested quietly. "But you might be able to help us. These people know you, and trust you, especially the women. Perhaps they will talk to you while they refuse to talk to us."

Her face was instantly angry again. "What do you expect me to do — refuse to help that poor expectant mother until she tells me all that she knows?"

"Don't be a bloody fool!" Mason exploded angrily. "All I ask is that you ask a few tactful questions of the other women in the village. Can't you understand that if those village men pull another trick like the one they pulled this morning then the next time they might not be so successful. They might be the ones to get massacred and not the Chinese. If you really want to help them then you'll help us to prevent it." He drew a deep, angry breath and then concluded. "But obviously you don't want to understand. You prefer to bury your head in the sand and pretend that the war isn't even happening. I'm sorry that I bothered you." He turned his back on her and walked swiftly away.

"Captain Mason!" She called him back and he stopped. Her face was troubled but after a moment she inclined her head slowly. "I will ask them — after I have

89

treated my patient."

Mason relaxed, and then smiled. "Thank you."

She nodded briefly and then disappeared into the stone house.

Mason rejoined the rest of his party and found that the big Sergeant had now questioned all of the village men, and had extracted nothing but a reluctant admission that a stranger had brought the guns to them on a mule. They returned to the headman Tarong but despite the big Sikh's efforts and some bland bullying from Panjit Sangh Tarong remained adamant. The guns had been brought by a stranger. The village men had not paid for them. No one knew from where the stranger came, or where he went. That was all. Tarong denied that the men from Ladrung had attacked the Chinese but the rifles had all been used recently and it was obvious that he was lying.

For another half-hour Marijani attempted to argue some more solid facts from the villagers, picking men out of the line at random, and finally he had to confess that without resorting to rough treatment it would be impossible to get them to talk. Radhaven conferred briefly with Mason and Sangh and then decided that for the moment there was nothing he could do except confiscate the arms and scare the villagers as much as possible. To arrest them was impractical because there were no soldiers to spare to guard them and nowhere to house them. Mason expressed the hope that Karen Langford would be able to bring them some information and Radhaven's frustration was slightly appeased.

The hoard of arms were being stacked aboard the lead lorry when Mason saw the Doctor returning. Radhaven and Sangh followed him as he moved apart from the troops to meet her. She shook her head regretfully as she stopped in front of them. Her eyes were on Mason.

"I tried," she said simply. "But at the moment they are all too angry and resentful of your soldiers — and scared of their own menfolk."

Radhaven's lips tightened bitterly. Panjit Sangh shrugged.

Mason said quietly. "Thank you for trying."

She hesitated, then said: "I may still be able to help you. I have delivered the child, but I shall have to come out again to check on the mother in two days time. By then their ruffled feelings will be soothed and there will be no troops to upset them with guns. I think that then the women will talk to me."

Radhaven brightened. "That will be appreciated, Doctor. Anything you can discover will help." He seemed to recall his impolite attitude when she had arrived and attempted to make amends. "I notice that you are driving your own jeep now that you have lost your orderly. May I loan you one of my men to drive you back to Tagantse?"

She hesitated, and then accepted.

"Then I will arrange it." Radhaven moved off to give the order.

Mason barred the Doctor's way for a moment and asked seriously:

"What was it?"

She stared at him blankly, and then her smile flashed and showed that the last breach was healed. "It was a boy," she said. "And both of them are very well."

★ ★ ★

The next development came that night as Mason worked over a report to Alan Kendall in his billet. After returning from Ladrung he had spent the afternoon in a return visit to the Tagantse prison compound. Panjit Sangh had accompanied him and after confronting the two Chinese prisoners for the second time they had extracted the story that both of the men had found the rifles in their possession on the battlefield. They had picked them up as souvenirs and had been using them instead of their normal army-issued sten guns. After the morning's episode Mason felt inclined to believe them and ordered their return to the compound with their companions. Now he was trying to make sense out of the incidents for his report and was almost relieved to hear a sharp knock on his door. He opened it in his shirt-sleeves, expecting to find Panjit Sangh, and was surprised to find Karen Langford.

She smiled at him. "You look startled, I am sorry."

Mason relaxed and returned the smile. "I am surprised, but pleasantly so. What can I do for you?"

"I think I have some information for you. It is sooner than I expected."

The charm dropped away from him and he was instantly alert.

"You've been back to that village?"

She shook her head. "No, Captain. One of the villagers has come to see me. He wants to talk, but I think he expects to be paid for what he knows for he is deliberately evasive. But he did tell me one thing to prove his good intentions." She paused, as though expecting disbelief. "He said that the man who brought the guns had a shaven head."

Mason blinked. "A shaven head?"

"That's right. He wouldn't say any more so I told him to wait outside the camp until I return with you. It was plain what he wanted so I promised that you would pay him for his information."

She looked uncomfortable. "I suppose you will?"

Mason smiled. "I will if it's worth it. Give me two minutes to find my jacket and revolver and then lead the way to your fine mountain Judas."

6

The Mystery of Karakhor

The villager from Ladrung was hidden beneath a cluster of trees behind the sprawling encampment of army tents that had been erected beside Tagantse. Karen Langford led Mason in a wide circle around the encampment, and after fifteen minutes they reached the trees. She called softly and there was a nervous, shuffling sound from the area of densest shadow. She spoke again and the sound came nearer, and Mason recognized the outline of a man. They moved into the darkness to meet him and Mason's hand stayed close to the unbuttoned flap of his revolver holster. He was wary of a trap but his senses brought no sign of danger and he relaxed when he was satisfied that the villager was alone.

In the darkness only the man's eyes were visible, they were wide and nervous in the black blob of his face. His outline was small and stooped and the only definite thing about him was a strong, unwashed smell. He cowered at Mason's approach but a soft word from Karen made him stand his ground.

Mason reached into his pocket and picked out the largest coins. He jangled them in his hand and then opened his palm so that the silver glinted dully.

"Tell him that this is all for him if he will tell me where his people obtained those arms. And reassure him that there will be no reprisals on his village."

Karen translated the words softly and the villager reached hesitantly for the money. Mason's fist closed sharply.

"Tell him to talk first."

Karen spoke again, and after a moment the villager answered her, his voice coarse and fretful. They argued in whispers and then Karen turned to Mason.

"He says that the rifles were brought to the village by a stranger with a mule, and that they were given freely and with no demand for payment. The stranger told them how the Chinese have robbed, raped and burned during the invasion of Tibet and warned them that the same would happen to their own village if they did not fight. The stranger told terrible stories of Chinese cruelties, and especially of their violation of monasteries and their ill-treatment of holy monks." She paused and then added her own conclusions. "It sounds as though this man whipped them up into a frenzy of fear and goaded them into attacking the Chinese. They are simple, superstitious people who can be easily incited."

"This stranger," Mason said. "Was he the man with the shaven head?"

Karen turned back to question the villager but this time the man's reaction was withdrawn. Mason guessed at the reason and unclosed his fist, allowing half of the silver coins to fall into the eagerly outstretched hand of the informer. The man began to speak again.

"It is the same man," Karen translated. "He wore long hooded robes and endeavoured to keep his face hidden while he talked to Tarong and the other men of Ladrung. But when he began to issue the rifles from the back of his mule the hood slipped back and revealed the shaven head."

Mason allowed another coin to pass into the shaking hand before him. His eyes were more accustomed to the thick darkness caused by the surrounding trees and he could distinguish the look of greed on the man's face.

"Ask him where the man came from?"

Karen obeyed but the only answer was a quick head-shaking gesture that seemed to waft the scent of sweat and dirt closer to Mason's nostrils. The man's feet shifted nervously through the rustling carpet of leaves.

Karen said: "He doesn't know. The stranger had never been to the village before. He came down from the mountains and returned the same way."

Mason closed his fist over the few coins left in his palm.

"Get him to be more explicit. I want to know exactly from which direction our gun-toting stranger came."

Karen questioned the man again, but this time he was unwilling to answer.

He gestured evasively and stepped back deeper into the trees. Mason's eyes narrowed as he recognized the increasing fear the hill-man conveyed and he held out the last of the coins temptingly. Finally, with great reluctance, the man uttered a name.

"Karakhor," Karen repeated it sharply, glancing at Mason's face. "He says the stranger came from the direction of Karakhor."

"Where's that? Another village?"

"No." Her tone was puzzled. "It's a lonely monastery high in the mountains behind Ladrung, the home of a colony of Buddhist monks."

"And the stranger who brought the arms had a shaven head," Mason mused thoughtfully. "Could he have been a monk?"

Karen put the question to the villager but the man was too frightened of his own admission to co-operate any further. He winced at the very name of Karakhor. Finally the Doctor turned back to Mason and said wearily:

"I don't think he is going to talk any

more. He seems to think that he has said too much already, certainly more than he had intended to say."

"All right." Mason gave the man the rest of his money. "Thank him and tell him that he can go."

The man needed no urging and Karen had barely finished speaking before he turned and dodged away through the trees. Almost immediately he was swallowed by the darkness and they were alone.

"What will you do now?" Karen asked.

Mason thought about it for a moment. "Find Lieutenant Sangh," he said at last. "And then take the story to either Radhaven or Colonel Rao and see what develops."

* * *

They found Panjit Sangh in the officers' mess and the young Lieutenant listened with interest to a condensed account of the informer's story. When Mason had finished he agreed that it should be repeated to one of his more senior officers, but was of the opinion that Samdar Rao would be too busy with the wider aspects of fighting the war and suggested that Radhaven was the man to approach. Mason agreed in turn and all three made their way to the Major's billet.

They found Radhaven alone but for an orderly who was promptly dismissed. The tall Major insisted that Karen take the only chair in the spartan room he occupied in one of the commandeered houses and Mason and Sang accepted an invitation to relax on the edge of the bunk-like bed. Radhaven turned on to its side the orange box he had been using as a crude table and used it as a fourth seat while Mason repeated the story he had just told Panjit Sangh.

The Major's sharp face darkened when Mason had finished and he said angrily: "Why wasn't this informer brought here to me?"

The reaction was unexpected but Mason was unruffled.

"If we had brought him here, he would not have talked," he pointed out reasonably. "I had to go outside Tagantse to meet him, and even then he only talked reluctantly."

Radhaven still glared at him. "All the same, I should like to have talked with this man. Since we left Ladrung this morning I have been feeling that we were too lenient with these people. This morning's events seem to connect vaguely with other matters that have troubled us recently, but I did not sense the connection until I had taken time to think more deeply and make certain investigations. I have a strange presentiment that this comparatively unimportant matter of a few villagers receiving arms may have strong implications."

Mason said quietly: "Can you explain, Major?"

Radhaven glanced hesitantly at Karen Langford, his expression registering doubt of anyone who was not an officer and a soldier. And then, as though accepting that her knowledge and contact with the hill people could be a continued asset, he pushed his scruples aside.

"I will try, Captain Mason. A few

days ago a patrol of our Sikh troops was ambushed in the hills along the battlefront. Not an uncommon occurrence during a time of war, I must admit, but it was in an area which we were practically certain was free of Chinese penetration. We could not discover exactly what had happened because every man in that patrol was killed."

Radhaven paused. "Can you see the connection that gradually filtered into my mind after we had left Ladrung, Captain. The circumstances were very similar to those surrounding the ambush of the Chinese truce party this morning. The idea worried me, and so I checked back on some of the past reports from the battlefront. I found yet another instance of one of our patrols being completely wiped out in an area which was believed to be free of Chinese. And what is more significant, there are three reports of small Chinese patrols being found shot dead in the hills for which we are certain no Indian troops were responsible."

Mason's jaw had tightened and Panjit Sangh looked frankly startled.

Then Karen Langford burst out incredulously. "But surely you can't believe that the village men of Ladrung have been carrying out murderous attacks on both sides, Chinese and Indian?"

Radhaven shook his head. "No, Doctor, I don't believe that the Ladrung villagers are wholly responsible. But I do think that the attack this morning fits into some hidden overall pattern. It seems to me that someone is deliberately attempting to fan the flames of war along this sector, someone who cares little how many men are killed, or on which side. Someone with some twisted desire of their own to simply watch the slaughter continue. Somewhere I believe there is a mind of evil and that the arming and organizing of the Ladrung villagers is merely a part of the main scheme of events."

The expression *mind of evil* seemed to linger in the room, tightening faces, and even the violence-tuned mind of Paul Mason became sensitive to a faint shiver.

Then Panjit Sangh said slowly. "These incidents of dead patrols, have they been confined to any particular area, Major?"

Radhaven nodded. "Loosely, yes. They all occurred along the stretch of the battlefront that lies close to Ladrung, and — " He paused to give emphasis to his next words. "And the monastery of Karakhor."

Mason remembered the fear on their informer's face when he had refused to reveal any more about that same name, and said bluntly: "I'm becoming very interested in this monastery. What can you tell me about it?"

Radhaven shrugged and his glance passed the query on to Karen Langford.

She looked uncomfortable. "I don't really know anything. Two years ago I was very welcome up there and I knew the Abbot very well. Then there was a bad outbreak of diphtheria in the region and by the time it was over I had a breakdown due to overwork. I spent several months in Delhi convalescing, and when I returned my reception had changed. I was still accepted by the bulk of my practice in the villages, but I was no longer welcome at Karakhor. The village people seemed to be afraid of the place and there was a strange veil of secrecy that I could never penetrate. It is often difficult to understand religious peoples and so I simply stopped my visits to the monastery and concentrated on the rest of my practice."

Mason frowned as he listened.

"Have you any idea what caused the change in their attitude? Did your Abbot friend give you any reason?"

Her olive eyes reflected perplexity. "I have no idea at all. And after my return from Delhi the Abbot would never receive me."

Mason said flatly: "Then I think that we should take a good look at this monastery of Karakhor. It seems to be crying out for investigation."

Radhaven's reaction was again unexpected, a complete reversal of his previous attitude. He said dubiously:

"I don't think we're justified in interfering with Karakhor, just because the man who brought the guns to Ladrung vanished in that general direction. The Buddhist religion has a very strong hold in

India and we could easily offend religious principles. I could not order my troops to search a holy place.

Mason was baffled for a moment, and then guessed that Radhaven must have firm religious principles of his own that made him shy away from any suggestion to approach the monastery.

He said tactfully: "Perhaps I could visit Karakhor alone."

"But what could you do? If Doctor Langford cannot get these people to talk then they most certainly will not oblige you. So what purpose could you achieve except to offend the local people and the monks?"

Mason tried to inject a note of reason. "You spoke of a mind of evil," he pointed out. "And you believe that whoever organized the Ladrung villagers is also responsible for wholesale murder along the battlefront. Surely that, and the fact that the man with the shaven head is more likely to be a monk than anything else, provide good reasons for investigating that monastery?"

Radhaven made no answer and Mason

searched for an ally. Panjit Sangh avoided his gaze and he saw that the Lieutenant sided with his senior officer. Karen was equally silent. Damn these Indians, Mason thought, and the same with religion. He tried again.

"The man had a shaven head. That signifies a monk. And there is a shroud of mystery over this monastery. We must find out what is going on."

Radhaven said angrily: "But I cannot trespass on sacred ground — and neither can I allow you to do so. A monastery is a holy place. It's inmates are holy people. And I cannot believe that a religious order could be responsible for the unexplained incidents I mentioned earlier."

Mason felt baulked, and wondered for a moment whether he would be justified in going above the Major's head and approaching Samdar Rao. And then Karen interrupted.

"Can we not compromise on this as before. When I visit Ladrung again I will attempt to learn some definite facts about Karakhor. If I press them I think the women will talk to me, they trust me more than the men. And then if it is warranted I can perhaps find some excuse to visit the monastery and Captain Mason can drive my jeep and accompany me." She smiled at Radhaven. "I'm sure the Captain will promise not to take any chances of offending the monks and simply act as an observer. Afterwards we can discuss the matter again before making any decisions."

Panjit Sangh smiled quickly. "That sounds sensible. I am inclined to agree."

After a moment of hesitation Radhaven gave a dubious nod of approval, and with that Mason had to be satisfied.

★ ★ ★

Later, as Mason walked the Doctor back towards her clinic he took the opportunity to thank her for her help. She looked at him strangely, her eyes mirroring the starlight, and then said:

"I suppose I must have seemed unreasonable last night, and again this morning at Ladrung."

"A little," he conceded the fact with

a smile. "But beautiful women do have certain privileges. That's one of them."

She was still ill-at-ease. "Perhaps I should explain."

"Only if you really want to."

They had reached her door and she turned to face him.

"I do want to." She hesitated. "As you can see, my mother was an Indian woman, but my father was a British officer. Our home was in the Brahmaputra valley. When the war came I was not very old, and my father left home to become one of the first to be parachuted behind the Japanese lines in Burma. He was captured and interrogated." Her voice remained steady. "And he died under that interrogation. A companion who was with him later escaped and described to my mother what had happened. She died of grief."

Mason said nothing, waiting for her to continue.

"I no longer have any real bitterness," she went on quietly. "For it was all so long ago. But the subject of interrogation, it — it still arouses a sense of blind anger.

So often the victim has nothing to tell. Can you understand?"

Mason nodded soberly. "Yes. I can understand."

"Thank you, Captain — " She stopped abruptly, and then made an effort to meet his eyes. "But it's Paul, isn't it?"

Mason smiled, his hands rested on her arms and he kissed her very gently on the lips. She stood rigid, and then her head turned slightly to one side and her mouth pressed closer. He held her properly then and felt the warmth of her body moulding against him and the sudden quick lift of her breasts. For a moment her mind was closed as she accepted and answered the movement of his lips, and then reluctantly she drew away.

"Good night, Paul. I must go now."

He released her. "Good night, Karen."

And then the rogue in him lifted her hand and lightly kissed the back of her wrist. A gallant, smiling gesture that seemed to both surprise and please her before she turned away.

7

The Room of Death

The violent hand on his shoulder was familiar in its urgency and Mason knew even before he opened his eyes that it belonged to Panjit Sangh. He noted that this time the young Indian had delayed to button his jacket correctly and that his smooth, dark face, although grim, was not as taut with anxiety as before. Sangh straightened up and Mason killed the first swift response of his reflexes and momentarily relaxed again.

"What now, Lieutenant? Have the Ladrung villagers attacked Command Headquarters? Or are the Chinese bowling atom bombs down the mountainside?"

Sangh's perfect teeth appeared in a deferential smile.

"It's not quite that bad, Captain. But disturbing news nonetheless. A village boy from Ladrung has just been brought in by

113

a sentry who stopped him approaching the camp. He says that there has been a murder in the village. A man named Ayyar has been found dead." He paused. "I think we can guess who this unfortunate Ayyar must be?"

Mason's body stiffened and he sat up slowly. He stared at Sangh but for the moment saw only the memory of the vague outline of a stooping man in the thick blackness below the trees behind the army camp. He remembered the man's fear; fear that had only wavered fractionally in his greed for silver. How much was the handful of silver worth to him now?

Mason pushed the thought down, becoming cold and professional as his gaze focussed on Panjit Sangh.

"How did he die?" he demanded. And although the words tasted bitter no trace of it showed in his tone.

Sangh shrugged. "The boy simply said that it was murder. He was taken to Major Radhaven and was apparently too frightened to make much sense. Radhaven wants us both to come along to Command Headquarters at once."

Mason was already lacing on his boots and he nodded briefly without looking up. He had slept fully clothed except for his jacket and revolver, for here on the front line with the Chinese pressing hard a break-through could mean that Tagantse might have to be promptly evacuated. So now he was ready in a minimum of time.

They reached Command Headquarters and were shown into a side room where Radhaven stood talking to the huge Sikh Sergeant, Marijani. The tall Major looked rake-thin beside the big bearded man but the Sikh was listening attentively. At the table behind them sat a small boy of about ten wearing a grubby, one-piece garment that was a cross between a sack and a nightshirt. The boy was eating from a bowl of rice but he stopped with his fingers still dipped among the grains and his eyes wary as Mason and Sangh entered.

Radhaven broke off his conversation and said grimly:

"Good morning, Captain. Events seem

to be developing in Ladrung. I assume that Lieutenant Sangh has told you what has happened?"

Mason nodded. "A murder."

"Quite so. And who would you suspect to be the victim?"

Mason scented the note of accusation in Radhaven's voice, as though his dealing with the man had been the definite cause of death. He said flatly: "My informer. What happened exactly?"

Radhaven glanced at the boy, who still remained in his frightened, open-mouthed pose.

"He cannot tell us. It seems that his mother discovered the body and sent him here to us. To find any actual details means another visit to Ladrung." His expression was faintly hostile as he went on. "But this time you and Lieutenant Sangh will have to go without me. Last night the Chinese attacked heavily on our right flank and gained several miles in contested territory. The action cost us over one hundred and fifty men in dead, wounded and prisoners. In an hour we launch a counter attack and

I will be needed here at Headquarters. Colonel Rao has given orders that you and Lieutenant Sangh must act on your own resources. The Ladrung villagers and the stolen rifles are your mission, Captain Mason, but for the moment the threat of the Chinese advance must have our full attention here."

Mason said gravely: "I understand, Major."

Radhaven's gaze flickered over him sharply, as though searching for some sign of irony. Mason suspected that the tall Major was more disturbed than he cared to admit about the mystery surrounding Ladrung and the monastery beyond, and that he did not welcome having to stand back and leave the investigations to another. Especially to an Englishman who might not respect the religious immunity of the monks. A moment later his suspicions became facts as Radhaven said bluntly:

"Please remember that no matter what develops at Ladrung you are not to go on to Karakhor without first consulting me." He waited for a sign of acceptance and then relaxed a little. "Sergeant Marijani will accompany you, Captain. Frankly I should not spare him, but he speaks the local dialect fluently and will be invaluable to you. I can also allow you a four man escort in case of trouble, but that I am afraid is all." He straightened his shoulders and concluded. "And now I must get back to the central command room and report to Colonel Rao. I wish you luck."

Mason waited until the door had closed behind Radhaven's tall figure, and then turned his attention to the village boy from Ladrung. Panjit Sangh moved closer to the table but the youngster simply looked scared and backed away as the Lieutenant tried to speak. Sangh hesitated, and then Marijani said softly:

"If you please, sir, I will speak with him. His name is Nadar and he trusts me a little." The white gleam of his teeth was accentuated by the flowering black beard and he explained briefly. "I have three of my own, sir. One of them just like this — except cleaner of course."

Mason grinned and nodded approval.

He and Panjit Sangh watched as the big Sergeant approached and spoke to cowering Nadar. The boy's dirt-smudged face remained blank for a moment, and then unexpectedly he smiled. Marijani returned the smile broadly, and then ruffled the boy's tangled hair. Then confidently the Sikh stood upright, lifted the boy with ease on to one square shoulder, and reported that Nadar was ready to go home to his village.

Mason grinned an acknowledgement and led the way out of the building to where the four men Radhaven had promised were all waiting in two jeeps. Two minutes later they were on their way back to Ladrung.

★ ★ ★

They entered the village in a cloud of dust stirred by the wheels of the jeeps, having made fast time through the hills without the two heavy lorries to slow them down. Their arrival seemed to be expected for most of the villagers were standing in the open to watch them.

Mason guessed that the woman who had found the body must have aroused the village after sending her son to fetch the army, and he wondered if the boy would have been allowed to leave if she had roused the men first. Judging from the hostile faces the answer was no.

He climbed out of the jeep on to the dusty ground and Panjit Sangh joined him. Both of them had unsnapped the flaps on their revolver holsters but the villagers made no move to cause them to draw the weapons free. Their driver, another Sikh, had a submachine-gun across his back, but he sat impassively at the wheel and waited for orders.

The second jeep drew up with Marijani and the remaining three soldiers, again all turbaned Sikhs. The boy Nadar was still perched high on the Sergeant's shoulder, and had been there throughout the ride. Despite the rough track and the fierce jolting of the jeep he had been completely trusting to the big man's firm grip. Now he was showing signs of nervousness again as he sensed the mood of his elders.

Marijani got out of the jeep, still supporting his human burden and with a rifle in his free hand. Two of the soldiers followed him with submachine-guns, while the driver remained at the wheel.

Mason said calmly: "You can return little Nadar to his mother, Sergeant. I don't think we need worry him any more."

Marijani nodded, and then bowed his broad back to lower the boy to the ground. Nadar looked hesitant, and then the Sikh's gleaming, black-framed grin showed reassuringly and a bar of chocolate was produced from the breast pocket of the outsize army tunic. Marijani gave the boy both the chocolate and a gentle push and sent him running towards a frightened woman with flying black hair who instantly enveloped him in the folds of her skirts.

Mason and Sangh had already approached the unsavoury Tarong. The headman's face showed no signs of welcome and he spat on the ground as they stopped in front of him. Marijani came towards them and now his face was stern again. The magnificent beard and flashing eyes denoted pure warrior blood as he glared at Tarong.

Mason said grimly: "Tell him that we want to see the body of this Ayyar who was murdered."

Marijani repeated the demand in the local tongue and Tarong shifted sullenly. Finally he turned and gestured to a gap between two of the crude stone huts. Marijani snapped an order and after a moment's hesitation the headman turned to lead the way.

The two soldiers started to follow but Marijani waved them back. He held his own rifle in a manner that stated he was quite capable of protecting the two officers in his charge from the whole village of Ladrung, and the Chinese Army as well if the need arose. Mason measured the man's size again and decided that Marijani would be an asset in any kind of corner.

They passed between the two stone buildings and circled a pair of tethered goats. There was a strong smell of drying dung from the flat roof-tops and a general air of disrepair. A wall had fallen down and they had to climb over the rubble to continue. Then they reached the far side of the small village, and here Tarong stopped by the door of one of the huts. He pointed grudgingly and then stood aside.

Mason went in with Panjit Sangh close behind him. Marijani stayed by the door, his attention on the headman who began to scratch beneath his rough sheepskin jacket and stare down at his sandaled feet where the grimy toes splayed from beneath the leather straps. They were conscious of the hidden women staring from the darkened interiors of the surrounding huts.

Inside the hut the light was dim. It came through a single window opening and through the doorway behind them in two angled streams of sunlight that met like a spotlight in the centre of the floor. Dust hung thick and still in the light, but beyond its range the room was dark. The stone walls were bare and the floor was hard-packed earth. There was a rough wooden chair and a low bed at the far end of the room. A few cooking and eating utensils hung from some roughly fashioned shelves of orange-box wood against one wall.

Almost immediately Mason heard the buzzing of the flies, and then he saw them like an evil cloud above the vague shape half covered by the blankets on the bed. He went closer but the body told him nothing except that he wanted to be sick. It looked as though at least a dozen blows from a heavy club had been needed to make the present mashed mess of the man's head.

He heard Panjit Sangh's indrawing breath beside him and heard the scrape of his shoes on the earth floor as he recoiled. But he didn't look. Instead he pulled the blankets back from the huddled body and stared more closely in the gloom. The figure was small, most probably would have been stooping in life, and he was almost certain that this was his informer from last night. Then he saw the glitter of silver coins lying beside the dead hand and the last doubt vanished. He half turned his head to speak to Panjit Sangh, and then suddenly there was a soft rustle of movement in the blankets by the body. He looked back sharply and in the same instant a hideous black head rose hissing into his face.

Mason froze, staring into the glittering eyes of death. Death swayed, poised for the blinding lunge of movement that no man alive would be fast enough to avoid. Panjit Sangh recoiled in horror and Mason crushed the overpowering urge to blink and shut out the sight of death. Death was hesitant, but the flicker of even an eyebrow would end all hesitation. Sweat drenched and became ice-cold over Mason's face.

Marijani heard Sangh's gasp of terror and spun round in the doorway, the rifle automatically lifting in his hands. He saw Mason crouching by the bed and for a second he could not understand why the Britisher's body had become rigid. And then the gleam of the eyes betrayed the ugly hooded head of the cobra only inches away from Mason's face. Marijani took the risk of shooting his officer in the back of the head without hesitation, flinging up his rifle for a lightning swift shot.

The bark of the rifle seemed to explode inside Mason's head and a red hot iron seared across his cheek. The impact threw him aside and in the same second the flaring head of the cobra flew into a shredded mess before his eyes.

For one horrible moment Marijani thought that he had killed Mason as the Marine Captain fell, and then he saw that Mason was clutching at his cheek. Marijani sprang towards him and then Panjit Sangh let out another yell as a second cobra appeared from beneath the bed. The young Indian seized the crude chair, the only furniture in the hut and lashed out as the snake struck. Venom splashed in milky drops as the lunging fangs hit the chair leg, and then Marijani slammed his rifle butt in a crushing blow that pinned the second flaring hood to the stone wall. The big Sergeant struck twice more and then relaxed.

Mason struggled to his feet, still caught between the sick fear that had frozen him to the spot, and inadvertently saved his life, and the burning agony of his creased cheek. Marijani moved to help him, while Panjit Sangh pulled his revolver and looked nervously for more snakes.

Mason managed to talk and said feebly: "I don't think there'll be any more, Lieutenant. One must have been put here deliberately, the other probably came to join its mate."

Sangh licked his lips. "Then this was an attempt to murder?"

"That's right." Mason spoke through pain-twisted lips. "Whoever killed Ayyar must have realized that once the body had been discovered the villagers would not come near this room again. So after the discovery he popped back with a little welcoming committee for us." Anger was raging through him now and combating the pain and he pushed away from Marijani. "Let's go, Lieutenant. I'm going to tear this place apart until I find out who and why."

8

Strange Rumours

They left the room of death and returned to the sunlight. Tarong had vanished and Mason swore, but after a moment they heard a violent stream of protest and the headman appeared again, backing away from the threatening submachine-guns of the two Sikh troops who had stayed by the jeeps. The soldiers stopped their running advance as they saw their three officers all upright and alive by the door of the hut. Tarong fell over backwards and lay on a heap of rubble, chattering with fear.

Marijani called a brief explanation to his men and the two soldiers relaxed. Tarong was ordered to his feet and ushered roughly back towards the jeeps. Mason, Panjit Sangh and Marijani followed. Sangh still held his revolver and looked as though he would dearly love to use it.

Mason's cheek still stung with agony, but a brief inspection by Sangh assured him that the bullet, although fanning close enough to burn a livid weal, had not actually cut the flesh. Marijani snapped an order and procured some greasy yellow butter from one of the village women which was gently smeared over the burn. The grease soothed and the sting abated enough for Mason to turn his thoughts elsewhere.

He said gratefully: "That was an excellent shot, Sergeant. Thank you."

Marijani smiled. "I was the rifle shooting champion of my regiment, Captain, long before I was promoted to Sergeant."

Mason nodded, and then turned so that his words included Panjit Sangh.

"That dead man was the informer who came to me last night. Whoever battered his head in left the silver I paid over beside the body, either as a warning to the other villagers not to take bribes, or to warn me not to offer them."

Panjit Sangh still held his revolver and now he slapped the barrel in the palm of his hand in an angry gesture. "I think it is time that this illiterate village realized that we have no time to play games. This man must talk!"

He pointed to the cowering Tarong by aiming the revolver. The headman scrambled backwards and then turned, only to have a submachine-gun jammed into his chest. Mason's mood was beyond pity for the man's ignorance and he simply nodded in agreement.

Marijani towered over the headman and barked questions in a voice like thunder. Tarong made denials and one of the Sikh troops cut him to his knees by slamming the butt of his gun across the calves of the man's legs. Panjit Sangh's revolver stabbed like a pointing finger against the dirt-streaked forehead.

There was a mutter of anger from the villagers and automatically the remaining Sikh soldier turned to face them with his gun cradled in his arms. The two drivers who had remained with the jeeps impassively unslung their own weapons.

Marijani's voice boomed again. Tarong jabbered in terror. Panjit Sang thrust hard with his revolver, pushing the man's head to one side until the barrel skidded off the sweating temple. A circular indentation showed clearly on the wretched man's forehead and he huddled suddenly on his knees, his arms thrown defensively around the back of his head.

Mason said grimly: "What does he say?"

"He claims that he does not know who killed Ayyar," Marijani answered. "He says he knew nothing of the murder until a woman, the mother of Nadar, aroused him in the night. And he pretends to know nothing of the snakes."

Panjit Sangh added flatly: "I think that he is the murderer. If it were anyone else he would turn them over to save his own skin." The young Indian's smile was bared in a savage gleam of teeth. "Let us take him into one of the huts, Captain, out of sight. He will talk."

Mason's cheek still stung and the memory of that evil black head rearing into his face was still clear, and the words of approval trembled on his tongue. Then he forced them back.

"No," he insisted. "Find the woman instead and talk to her. Find out whether she did send the boy straight to us when she found the body, or whether she was told to send him. If she was acting under orders then it's a fair assumption that whoever gave them also arranged for the cobra to be planted on the body."

Marijani nodded in acknowledgement. When he had released Nadar he had taken note of the woman who had scooped the boy into her skirts and now he quickly brought her forward from the crowd of watching villagers. There was a mutter of threats from the men but the big Sikh's handling of the woman was firm but gentle and no one interfered.

After a brief interrogation, which the woman answered in a low voice with downcast eyes, Marijani turned to report.

"She says that she found the body just before dawn. She heard a noise from Ayyar's hut which is next to her own, and as she is a widow with no husband she had to go herself to see what caused it. She spoke to Ayyar and when he did not answer she touched him. Her hand came away sticky with blood and she ran back to her hut. She was afraid, but after a while she roused the boy Nadar and sent him to Tagantse. Then she roused some friends and they awoke the headman. She says Tarong was angry when he heard that she had sent Nadar to tell the army."

Mason frowned. "Ask why Tarong was so angry?"

Marijani did so. The woman's eyes darted a scared look at the headman who still crouched on the ground, but after a brief hesitation she answered.

Marijani said: "She says that Tarong hates the army since they took his guns away yesterday. She knew this, but Ayyar had shown signs of asking her to be his wife and she wanted his murderer to be punished. That is why she sent Nadar to us."

Mason said slowly: "So the cobra on the body must have been an afterthought, put there by the murderer after dawn this morning when she had roused the village. Ask her if she has seen anyone enter the death hut since dawn?"

Marijani asked the question but the woman shook her head. She had seen no one enter or go near the hut. Mason suggested a few more questions but it was soon obvious that the woman could tell them nothing more and finally he released her.

Then began a repetition of the previous day, of pulling the villagers forward one by one to be subjected to Marijani's exhaustive questioning. And the process was equally frustrating. No one would admit to any knowledge of the murder. No one would admit to having seen Ayyar return from Tagantse, or to have seen anyone approach the death hut after it was learned that the army had been told. Nobody knew anything. The village had adopted a mantle of silence.

At the end of two baffling hours they had learned exactly nothing. Mason was sure that when Ayyar had returned from Tagantse he had either been questioned about his absence, or had been fool enough to reveal his ill-gotten silver; one of those reasons had led to his attack in the night. He was certain too that Tarong must be the killer, but he could not prove it.

Finally he had to face defeat, he could reconstruct the crime, but he could prove nothing. The defiant villagers just would not talk. Panjit Sangh favoured a fresh round of interrogation using more violent methods, but Mason had to remain firm. He had to remember that he was a British officer interfering in what was basically an Indian affair, and that if the affair managed to leak to the ears of anti-British politicians in Delhi then the stink might be considerable. He had to use the soft glove.

The drive back to Tagantse was galling, his cheek stung like fury and he boiled inwardly at the memory of Tarong's insolent grin when he had realized that for the moment he was free and had watched the two vehicle convoy drive away.

* * *

The heavy guns were creating their nightmare of sound again when the two

135

jeeps reached the front-line command post and it was plain that the Indian counter-attack had been launched against the swarming Chinese. Large mushrooms of smoke and dirt were blooming along the line of a five-mile distant ridge across the valley, but there seemed to be no immediate threat to Tagantse. A junior officer hurrying past informed them that the battle was momentarily too disjointed for anyone to know whether any real progress was being made but an air strike due to arrive at any moment should swing the odds on to the Indian side. It was obvious that they would not be welcomed inside Command Headquarters and so Mason dismissed Marijani and his four men, and then, accompanied by Panjit Sangh, made his way to Karen Langford's clinic.

She was alone and in the middle of packing as they entered. A large open trunk was on the floor and she was arranging a pile of medical books in the bottom. She looked up at the sound of the door.

"Hello, Paul — Lieutenant Sangh. I'm

just clearing out. I've been advised to transfer all my equipment to the next village south until the pressure is taken off this sector of the frontier. Most of the Tagantse people who form the largest part of my practice have already left anyway and — " She broke off suddenly. "Paul — your face!"

He gave a brief explanation of the morning's events and finished: "It's not serious, just a bullet hum, but it's starting to sting like fury again."

She turned his face to the light and winced. Then her medical training took over and she pushed him down to a chair. She found a hypodermic, changed the needle, and then filled the instrument from a small bottle. "This helps to kill the pain and stops infection," she explained as she made the injection close to the angry red weal.

Afterwards he took her wrist and said quietly: "Are you leaving immediately, Karen?"

She shook her head. "I'm moving a lot of my stuff, and keeping the rest ready-packed. But I've got one or two

137

sick patients in the villages, including that mother at Ladrung. I won't leave them until I have to."

"That what I was afraid of." He still gripped her wrist. "I didn't come here just for doctoring, Karen, but to warn you to stay away from Ladrung. Those hill men have really got something to hide, they're stubborn and they're surly, and the fact that they think they've got away with that murder this morning means that they'll have even less scruples about killing again. They're too dangerous."

She looked at him seriously. "But I shall have to visit that patient."

"All right, but forget about asking questions."

She smiled suddenly. "It won't be necessary. Ladrung isn't the only village in the area. This morning I was out at Seral, one of the places you visited first in your search for arms. Seral is as close as Ladrung to Karakhor, and one of the women there feels very much in my debt as I once saved her son during the diphtheria outbreak. I talked to her this morning, and I think she told me as much as anyone else would be able to tell."

Panjit Sangh came closer as Mason looked up sharply. In that moment a formation of Indian jet fighters swept low over the clinic as they roared towards the battlefront, but the thunder of their vibrations passed almost unnoticed.

Mason said tensely: "What did the woman say?"

Karen hesitated a little at the reaction of the two men. Then she said slowly: "I still have no concrete facts, but there are many strange rumours connected with Karakhor. There is a suggestion that the old Abbot whom I knew has died, but no one knows for sure and no one has seen his successor. The monks very rarely come down into the villages, and when they do they simply buy and sell, or whatever they have come to do, and evade all questions. They hurry back to Karakhor as quickly as possible and some strange mystery seems to shroud the whole monastery. My woman said that no villager from Seral has visited Karakhor for many months, and it seems that the local people are no more warmly received at the monastery than I am."

"Could she tell you anything about the villagers of Ladrung?"

Karen shook her head. "Nothing. A month ago there was the normal friendly relationship between Seral and Ladrung and the other villages. But the war and the fear of the Chinese has disrupted everything and now the people of Ladrung remain aloof."

Bees of frustration buzzed in Mason's brain. "Has there been any attempt to arm the Seral villagers?" he asked.

Karen shook her head. "I asked. If there had been my woman would have known and she would have told me. I am sure she was completely honest with me. And to the best of her knowledge there have been no arms distributed to any other village in the area."

Mason said helplessly: "So the affair is confined to Ladrung — that is to Ladrung and Karakhor. But as both Indians and Chinese have been attacked, where is the sense in it?"

Panjit Sangh said slowly: "Remember

that here we are on the borders of Tibet, Captain. When the Tibetans rose against the Communists to cover the escape of their holy leader, the Dalai Lama, in 1959, it was the monks who led the fighting. Many of them died and their monasteries were set ablaze. The hatred of the monks for the Chinese was almost equalled by their resentment of the Indians to whom they appealed unsuccessfully for help. The monks of Karakhor undoubtedly have strong religious connections with their brothers in Tibet. Perhaps they feel now that India is only getting what she deserves for leaving the Tibetans to their fate. That could provide a reason for their activities to be directed at both sides."

Mason thought hard, recognizing the strong grains of truth in the young Lieutenant's words, but still unable to accept it as the whole truth. He said at last:

"I could accept that if they had incited all the local villages. But they haven't. Only Ladrung. It can't be because they lack arms, because far more were stolen than we've recovered."

There was silence for a moment, and then Mason looked at Sangh.

"There is really only one answer, Lieutenant. We must go to Karakhor and find the facts."

Panjit Sangh looked uncomfortable. "I now incline to agree, Captain. But I cannot approach Karakhor in defiance of Major Radhaven's orders. And with a major battle in progress I doubt if he will spare time to listen to any new arguments." He looked even more uncomfortable and added apologetically: "I would also be failing in my duty, Captain, if I allowed you to visit the monastery in defiance of those orders."

Mason nodded slowly, as an army officer he knew that the young Lieutenant's hands were tied. Radhaven had insisted that he be consulted before any definite approach to Karakhor, and that was a direct order that Panjit Sangh could not disobey. Mason cursed the Major's religious scruples that made him dither over offending the monks, but for the second time that day he had to admit defeat.

★ ★ ★

For the rest of the day the battle raged in the hills to the north of Tagantse as the Chinese hurled wave after wave of reserve troops down the mountainside in an effort to stem the Indian attack. An evergrowing pall of twisting smoke hung over the ridge-tops and was frequently plastered by the Indian fighters that howled back and forth overhead. As far as Mason could understand the position had reached a deadlock, but the fighting continued and he received no chance to tackle Radhaven. Panjit Sangh was commandeered by a desperate Lieutenant Colonel to rush some despatches up to the front line, and Mason found himself in the awkward position of an unwanted observer. He spent the afternoon in helping Karen Langford to pack and in fretting over the problem of Karakhor.

By nightfall the guns were still playing hell and damnation along the battlefront, and he realized that he would not get a chance to see Radhaven until dawn at least. He ate a cold meal with Karen in the officers' mess and then escorted her back to the clinic.

For a moment he kissed her, but she was troubled and tired and after a moment pushed him away. He understood and bid her good night, she was not in love with him and at the moment the war was too close for her to enjoy any dalliance of lust.

He returned slowly to his billet, his mind still grappling with the baffling mask of silence surrounding the monastery. His initial assignment of tracing the stolen arms seemed to shrink into insignificance now, and how they had reached the Himalayas hardly mattered. The important question was why were the monks of Karakhor using them to fan the flames of violence along the already bloody battleground of the frontier? They were not selling the arms, so where was the motive?

He was still wondering as he reached his billet and opened the door. Inside was darkness and he closed the door behind him before lifting the torch he used to locate the single oil lamp. His finger was already squeezing on the torch button when a cold spear of warning triggered in his brain.

He hesitated, still in darkness, and then recognized the factor that his subconscious mind had sensed before him. The single window that he had left open for ventilation was now almost closed. He knew too that he was not alone.

His muscles worked purely by reflex. He moved swiftly to one knee, swayed his body to the right, and thrusting his left arm full length to his left clicked on the torch and shone the beam forward.

The strong beam brought the waiting man into focus as though projecting a film. He was tall and wearing the long, hooded robes of a holy monk. And then the ugly knife in his hand flashed in a streak of silver down the beam of light. Had Mason been holding the torch normally in front of him the blade would have scored a hit square in his chest. Instead it passed over the top of his outstretched wrist and smacked into the door. Mason's right hand was already pulling his revolver clear from its holster and he shot the man deliberately through the knee cap.

The monk screamed above the sound of the shot, twisting away as he fell. Mason smiled grimly with satisfaction and started to rise, lowering his revolver.

That was when the second hooded figure sprang at him from behind the door and he realized that, as with the coiled cobra, the first killer had a mate.

9

The Citadel of Fear

Mason twisted to meet the second man's attack and they collided heavily in the darkness. The force of the other's rush slammed Mason against the door and as he tried to bring his revolver up for a second shot crushing fingers clamped on his wrist and forced his hand away. The revolver roared but the bullet smashed harmlessly into the far wall. A second knife gleamed in the man's free hand, stabbing savagely downwards. Mason parried the blow with his torch and the impact snapped the thin blade and sent it spinning away. The torch flew from Mason's jarred fingers in the same moment and smashed on the floor, but not before he had seen that the hand gripping the useless knife hilt was thickly covered with dense black hair. Then he was fighting desperately for his life in the darkness.

Paul Mason was a strong man, in the peak of physical fitness, but immediately he recognized a superior strength. The hand gripping his wrist shifted to fasten over his knuckles and literally squeezed the revolver out of his cracking fingers. Mason gasped with agony and grappled helplessly. His free hand clawed at the other's face, the fingers gouging for the eyes. He missed, his fingers slipped down the face and then sought for the throat. This time he found his target, but the neck was massive and he could feel more covering hair. He tried to dig thumb and fingers round the windpipe and then both the man's arms wrapped around him and crushed. Mason's back arched and he screamed.

He had to release his grip on the throat in order to brace himself against the terrible pressure that threatened to snap his spine. The hooded man was bending over him, his panting breath blowing fully into Mason's face. They were only inches apart and the fetid gusts of air that almost choked him provided Mason with a clear guide, and lunging his face forward he snapped his teeth as hard as possible on the man's nose. The man screeched in agony and Mason exerted every ounce of pressure in his jaws, tasting blood before the other released his back-breaking hold and jerked away.

Every muscle in Mason's body cried out in pain, but he knew that if his powerful antagonist trapped him against the wall again he was done for. He twisted his shoulders away and gripped the front of the man's robes at the same time. He rolled backwards and brought his knee hard into the other's groin as the big man came with him. They hit the floor heavily and in the pitch darkness Mason misjudged his fall. His head connected with the foot of his own bed and a flash of light burst inside his brain. The light went out and Mason went out with it.

The hooded man struggled to his feet, half retching and half sobbing as he clutched both hands at his groin. Mason was silent but the man with the bullet-smashed knee-cap was groaning and whimpering on the floor. Outside men were shouting and rushing to the scene.

The hooded man pulled himself together and located his groaning companion. Without ceremony he hoisted the man on to his massive shoulders and the groaning stopped as the injured man fainted. The hooded man staggered from the pain that still stabbed through his belly, but his huge strength conquered and he pushed open the door and stumbled out with his burden into the night.

★ ★ ★

Mason was falling upwards. It was a weird sensation to be defying the force of gravity and something in the back of his mind told him it was impossible, but he continued to fall up towards the light. The layers of darkness peeled away and with a last frightening rush he reached the surface. Hard boards pressed into his back and dull pain filled his head. A shadow loomed over him and with an effort he opened his eyes.

Panjit Sangh knelt over him, a revolver in his hand. Behind Sangh stood a Sikh soldier, cradling the inevitable submachine-gun. The oil lamp threw a yellow glow over the room, glinting on a broken knife blade, the smashed glass of his torch, and finally on a small dark pool of blood where he had shot the first of his attackers down.

Panjit Sangh said grimly: "I'm sorry, Captain, but the confusion gave him a chance to get away. When the shots were heard it was thought that the Chinese had launched a sneak attack and there was one hell of a flap. So by the time it was realized that there wasn't going to be any more shooting and we started looking for a cause inside Tagantse he must have had a pretty good start."

Mason struggled to a sitting position and said weakly: "There were two of them, Lieutenant, both wearing long hooded robes — monk's robes. I shot one in the knee-cap so the other must be carrying him."

Sangh turned, still crouching, to relay

151

the descriptions to the soldier behind him. The man saluted and hurried out, and then Sangh helped Mason to his feet.

"If one of them is wounded we might still be in time to catch them," he said dubiously. "But I don't think so. It is now twenty minutes since the shooting, and if they were still in the limits of the town they would have been found. Unfortunately the situation on the battlefront is still all-demanding and there are no men to spare for a proper search."

Mason felt the lump on the back of his head and said bitterly: "The man I fought with had the strength of a bull — he wouldn't have any difficulty in carrying his friend away."

Sangh slipped his revolver back into his holster and said unhappily: "After the incident with the snakes at Ladrung this morning I should have realized sooner that the shots came from here. What did actually happen?"

Mason told him, retrieving his fallen revolver and removing the knife from the door as he talked. When he had finished Sangh's expression was grave.

"Did you get a good look at these two men?" the Indian asked.

Mason shook his head. "The torch was only on for a moment before it got smashed, and the rest of the fight was in darkness. Their faces were hidden under the cowls of their hoods." As he talked he remembered the hairy wrists and throat he had felt during his desperate struggle, but he said nothing of them. He had the feeling that Panjit Sangh would probably conclude that he was suffering from the crack he had received on the head if he tried to explain that his assailant had been more like an ape than a man.

A moment later a Sergeant appeared in the doorway and reported that there was no sign of the two monk-like figures in Tagantse. The hooded men had got clean away.

* * *

Shortly after dawn the next morning the howling discord of war eased along the

153

northern ridges and Mason learned that the battle that had surged back and forth all through the previous day and night had at last been won. The Chinese had been forced back from some of their captured ground. The news was offset by the fact that another major battle had been fought nearer the Burma frontier and here the Chinese had captured the village of Walong and forced the Indians to take up new positions ten miles south. Mason grimaced and knew that despite the victory here, in the overall pattern the Chinese were winning the border war.

His own mission was still at stalemate, for he could not contact anyone who could authorize him to approach Karakhor. Colonel Samdar Rao was unavailable and Radhaven had taken a patrol out during the night on some unspecified task and had not yet returned. Panjit Sangh, who had left him the previous night to report the cause of the disturbance to Command Headquarters, had also disappeared, and he guessed that the young Lieutenant must again have been commandeered for running despatches.

Mason prowled restlessly, seeking information, but respecting the fact that the Indian officers whom he did see hurrying to and fro were busy with more important matters than his own problems. His own military training, prior to his transfer to Naval Intelligence told him that he would not be welcome in Command Headquarters. He paid a hopeful visit to Karen Langford's clinic, but even the doctor was absent. The frightening racket of last night's guns had probably brought on a premature birth somewhere.

He returned to his billet and scowled down at the dark stain on the floor where an orderly had wiped the blood away. His head had stopped aching after a night's sleep, but the lump was still sore to touch. Now the mood of frustration was upon him again. He sat down and started to compose an up-to-date report for Alan Kendall, but how did you compose a factual report out of suspicions and rumours?

He was still brooding over what he had written when a jeep pulled to a stop outside his door half an hour later. He looked up and saw Karen Langford get out of the driving seat and come towards him. She was wearing a crisp white overall and there was a hint of urgency in her movements as she came through the open doorway.

"Paul," she smiled breathlessly. "I think I've got the kind of news you've been waiting for. Have you had a chance to talk to Major Radhaven yet?"

"No, I haven't." He stood up. "But what's this news? Where have you been?"

She smiled again at his eagerness. "One question at a time, Paul. I've been out to Seral again, I had a villager knocking on my door early this morning because his brother had chopped off a finger cutting firewood. But that's not the point. While I was there I learned that a party of monks had passed the village this morning just before first light. There were four of them, and they were carrying a fifth. And they were heading for Karakhor."

She paused for breath and then went on. "One of the Seral villagers spoke

156

to the monks, and they said that their companion had broken his leg in a fall among the rocks, and that they were taking him back to the monastery." She moved closer and gripped his arm. "This is our chance, Paul. Radhaven said that we could visit Karakhor provided I had a good excuse that would not offend the monks, and that you simply acted as driver and observer. I can go up there and offer to set that broken leg."

She looked at him strangely, suddenly sensing that something was wrong. Then he explained.

"The idea is sound, Karen, except that you wouldn't be allowed in to set that broken leg. The reason being that the monk your village friends saw being carried up to Karakhor hasn't got a broken leg. He's got a knee-cap smashed by a bullet." He watched the smile die on her face as he told her the rest of the story.

She said at last: "So that's what the noise was all about last night — I didn't realize." She inclined her head in a pang of conscience. "I get so accustomed to guns and explosions this close to the battlefront that they become routine. The shots woke me last night but when they were not repeated I went back to sleep again. I didn't think about you."

Mason smiled. "There's no reason why you should have done. The attack was the last thing I expected here in camp."

She nodded, and then looked up slowly. "Paul, does this really prevent us from going up to Karakhor? I agree that they won't allow me to treat the monk, but all that we really want is an excuse to go there without offending those who are not involved in this business. I'm sure the whole monastery can't be mixed up in it. I used to know so many of those holy men, and especially the old Abbot. If I could just speak to him — "

"If he's alive?" Mason reminded her.

She stopped, and then said flatly: "There's only one way to find out — isn't there?"

Mason turned away rather than be influenced by her determined eyes. He stared at the wall for a moment and his face was stiff and blank as his brain balanced the odds. The broken leg story, even though they knew it to be false, did provide them with a perfect excuse for visiting the monastery. Radhaven could make no objections in view of his earlier ruling. But after the attack last night he knew that at least some of the monks would not hesitate to kill him. It was his job to risk his own life — but could he justify gambling with the Doctor's?

He sought for an alternative, but even in view of the new facts he doubted whether Radhaven would supply him with an escort of troops. In fact, if Radhaven's respect for religion was really strong, he might even retract his previous decision. Mason had a shrewd suspicion that the sharp-faced Major had only given way on that point because he was convinced that such a situation as this would not arise. Radhaven knew that the monks of Karakhor would never call for the doctor of their own free will and had felt himself safe to make reasonable-sounding concessions.

Mason realized then that the only way to be sure of reaching Karakhor was to go now before Radhaven returned. He felt sure that Panjit Sangh would accompany him now that it would not be in direct conflict with his duty, but if he waited for the young Lieutenant to return he might delay for too long. Besides, if all the inhabitants of the monastery were involved and decided to murder them, then two revolvers would not be much more use than one. He turned then, very slowly, to face Karen Langford.

"It could be dangerous," he said. "Even for you! Very dangerous."

Karen smiled, recognizing that his own decision was made.

"We'd best go right away," she said. "There's still plenty of petrol left in the jeep, and my medical bag is still on the back seat."

★ ★ ★

Mason felt it prudent to avoid the rebellious villagers of Ladrung, and so they drove a less direct route, circling through the hills and passing through the descriptively identical village of Seral.

Karen waved to some of the people she knew but they did not stop. The road began to twist very steeply into the mountains, and after several hazardous miles joined the widened mule track that led from Ladrung to Karakhor. The general direction was west, but Mason had an uncomfortable feeling that they were edging closer to the battle area beyond the northern ridges. The big guns were unusually silent after the last big battle and he almost wished that they would open up again to give him his bearings.

Karen sat in the passenger seat beside him but said very little as they bounced over the stony ribbon of rough track. They had disagreed at the start over Mason's uniform, for Karen had suggested that he find some clothes more fitting for an orderly-driver. However, Mason had pointed out that as he spoke none of the Indian languages he could not possibly pass for anything other than what he was, and so he had not changed. He reasoned that as he could not hide his identity the uniform of a British officer might at least

161

command him a little respect.

The road was the worst over which Mason had ever attempted to take any vehicle, and several times he thought that they would have to get out and walk. At one point a minor landslide had spilled across the road where it passed through a narrow cut and he had to get out and clear several of the larger boulders out of the way before he could force the jeep around it. As they passed the roaring of their engine caused more of the finely-balanced rocks and shale to tumble down behind them and he swore as he realized that he would have to clear it again on the way back. The road turned another bend almost immediately and continued to climb steeply around the side of the mountain.

As the road climbed so the valley dropped away on their right, and they were able to see clear across the ridge tops to the rising, snow-capped giants of the Himalayas beyond. Somewhere down there in the valley and the hills were the Chinese and Indian battle positions, and although they were out of range it was disconcerting to think that they were probably being watched through binoculars by both sides.

The dizzy road continued to wind round the side of the mountain veering gradually south. Then it began to descend again towards the valley. Mason's arms were aching as he struggled to keep the wheel still and prevent the jeep from jumping off the road, and he had little time to study their surroundings as the view extended in a sweeping curve around the mountainside.

Then Karen said suddenly:

"There, Paul! That is Karakhor!"

Mason slowed the jeep so that he could concentrate on the direction of her pointing finger in safety. Several miles ahead a massive shoulder of the mountain thrust out into the valley, almost bridging it to join the hills beyond. The shoulder was a stony grey wilderness of bald rock and earth above the tree line far below, and on its highest point, silhouetted against a blue-grey sky was the grim outline of the monastery.

Even from here the grey walls and lofty

roofs had a sinister aspect, seeming to crouch in iron domination of the valley from the lonely heights. Mason felt a faint movement deep in his belly and began to understand the veil of secrecy that the local villagers had woven around this remote citadel in the vastness of the mountains. Its very being instilled an element of fear.

He stared towards it, realizing that to reach it the road must dip down into the valley and then rise again. The thought brought another twinge of uneasiness and he glanced at Karen.

"It looks dangerously close to the Chinese lines."

"Not really." She tried to sound confident. "The battlefront is not a ruler-straight line running east to west. Instead it loops like a river. Here it loops away from Karakhor."

Mason started the jeep going again and headed down into the valley, concentrating once more on the vicious mule-track conditions of the road.

"I hope you're right," was all he said.

Half an hour later they were climbing

again, and the monastery was looming directly ahead, a great grey square with roofs on many levels. The last hundred yards were so steep that Mason feared that the jeep might crash back down the hillside if the wheels once slipped, and it was like driving straight up to a fortress in the sky. The walls towered over them, and somewhat to his surprise he saw that the large wooden gates were open.

He drove straight through and then stopped the engine. The jeep fell silent and they gazed slowly around the great, empty courtyard of forbidden Karakhor.

10

The Voice of Evil

There was no sound, and the very stillness hung over the lonely monastery like a warning cloud. Mason could feel Karen becoming tense beside him, and there was an uncanny wriggling sensation at the back of his own neck. He kept his hands on the wheel where they could cause no alarm to any hidden watchers, and searched the pillared cloisters that encircled three sides of the stone-paved courtyard for any signs of life. There were none. In the dark shadows beneath the arcades grotesque stone statuettes glowered back at him from carved niches in pillars and walls, the representations of Buddha and other religious deities. But nothing lived.

Could Karakhor be deserted?

He voiced the question quietly to Karen and she shook her head.

"No, Paul. There were over thirty monks here when I was last made welcome, and they must be here now. Look in the four corners of the cloisters."

He looked, and saw smoking oil lamps half hidden by the pillars, each one placed in front of larger editions of the statues. Someone must have lit them. He strained his eyes to penetrate the black openings that marked the doorways beyond the pillars but saw nothing.

Karen opened the door of the jeep and got down on to the courtyard. Mason joined her, and after a moment's hesitation they walked forward to the main entrance behind the pillars directly ahead. Then as they reached the first line of pillars, a figure appeared in the open doorway.

A nervous muscle jumped in Karen's throat and she stopped. Mason crushed the desire to feel for the reassuring shape of his revolver and waited beside her. The monk stepped out into the cloisters, a tall man wearing a long orange robe, the hood pushed back to reveal a closely shaven head, and a dark, hostile face. He stared suspiciously at Mason and then addressed a question to Karen.

Karen answered, her voice steady. The monk folded his arms across his chest and spoke in firm, negative tones. Mason knew without waiting to be told that Karen had offered to set the leg of the man who had been hurt, and that as they expected the offer had been refused. It was up to Karen now to talk her way into the monastery.

For five minutes Karen argued with the polite, but adamant monk, her voice respectful but firm. The monk listened civilly without interruption, but the hostility in his eyes increased. Once he looked at Mason and again his voice took on a questioning tone, and the answer she made left him clearly dissatisfied. Karen's voice became suddenly angry, and then, just as Mason had come to the conclusion that there was no hope of being allowed a peaceful entry, the monk gave way. He made a gesture of invitation with obvious ill grace and turned to lead them inside.

They followed him down a narrow

corridor where more burning lamps and carved statues, this time carved from yellow butter, adorned the niches in the walls. Mason caught a glimpse of another orange robe passing the end of the gloomy passage, and then their guide directed them into a side room. Here a second monk faced them with startled eyes. The first man spoke quickly to explain, and the man edged past them and hurried away. The room was a bare cell except for the rush matting on the floor, and was poorly lit by smoking lamps and the filtered daylight that reached through the door. There were no windows. The monk sat down and crossed his legs in front of him on the matting, and slowly Karen, and then Mason, followed his example.

Karen said quietly: "I told him that we had come a long way because we had heard that one of the monks had broken a leg. I had to make a pretence of wanting to see the man and that was what most of the argument was about. Then I said that even if my help was not needed we still needed food and rest before we started

169

to go back. They can't refuse hospitality to pilgrims and travellers and so he had to bring us in here." She paused and then added: "On previous occasions I have been entertained in more sumptuous rooms than this and treated very well. But it looks as though he's invited us into the most inhospitable room he can find in the hope that we'll soon be glad to go."

Mason said quietly: "Ask after the Abbot's health, and any other monk you can remember by name."

Karen nodded and again began her infinitely polite conversation with the monk. The man made very few answers and Mason sensed that most of them were non-committal, but there was nothing that the Marine Captain could do about it except smile courteously each time the dark, unfriendly eyes moved in his direction.

After a few moments the second monk returned, bearing a small tray arranged with coarse cakes. A third monk followed with a tray of small cups of hot, greasy liquid. Karen accepted one of the cakes and a cup and Mason did likewise. Their host pointedly refrained from sharing the refreshment. The two servant monks stood back by the wall and waited.

The cakes were dry and unpalatable, and the repugnant liquid in the cups proved to be tea made with the addition of rancid butter. Mason shuddered at the taste, but they had begged refreshment and now they had to maintain appearances and accept it. Karen continued her efforts of tactfully questioning their host but was obviously making no progress. On one point she became insistent despite the monk's first blunt refusal, only to accept defeat when his attitude became dangerously angry. Mason knew instinctively that she had attempted to gain an audience with the Abbot and had failed.

For fifteen minutes Mason sat and forced down the cakes and tea, watched by the two attendant monks while Karen attempted to argue with their host. At last he swallowed the last of the crumbling, badly-baked flour, and almost immediately their host rose to his feet. Mason and Karen rose also and it was plain that the tea party was over. Karen's face was strained and Mason knew that there was nothing more that she could do.

They were escorted back to the courtyard, and Karen whispered an unhappy apology as they walked out into the sunlight. Mason gripped her arm reassuringly and murmured that she had done her best. His brain was searching desperately for some means of remaining in Karakhor without drawing his revolver and resorting to violence. It was simply too galling to get here and then be sent home without learning a single thing.

The monk who had acted as their host bid them a grave farewell from the cloisters and watched as they climbed into the jeep. Mason reached for the ignition key and then a slow smile eased his grim expression.

"Cheer up," he said softly. "We're not quite beaten yet."

She looked at him blankly, and then understood as he slipped the key back into his pocket. He pulled the starter and made the motor whirr for the benefit of the watching monk, repeating the procedure until the man started to walk angrily towards him. Then he got out quickly, made a helpless face, and went round to the front to lift the bonnet.

The monk stopped by the jeep, his face full of suspicion as he spoke to Karen. The Doctor got out of the jeep and began making lengthy apologies. Mason smiled to himself as he listened to the argument with his head buried earnestly in the engine. He was confident that the monk would not know enough about car mechanics to realize that there was nothing really wrong with the jeep, no matter how suspicious he might be. Chuckling softly to himself he decided that *repairs* would be a series of lengthy jobs that would last at least until dark. They could not be expected to drive that foul mountain road at night and the monks would have to extend their hospitality.

★ ★ ★

Throughout the long hot afternoon Mason conscientiously dismantled, cleaned, and reassembled as many parts of the jeep's engine as he could reach, his tools spread in businesslike array about the courtyard. He was watched continuously by a succession of monks who came and stood in angry silence in the shadow of the cloisters to watch him until relieved, but he ignored them while he concentrated virtuously on his *repairs*. Karen played up admirably, both in helping him to grope inside the engine and in maintaining her seemingly distressed apologies to the constant queries of the monks. At dusk they were still there, and the carburettor and the distributor were still in pieces, the carburettor for the third time.

Mason had managed to conceal his satisfaction as the sun had set beyond the golden sheen of the monastery roofs, but now he risked a tired smile as the shadows grew thick in the courtyard. Even the bright orange robe of their present guardian monk was barely visible in the darkness now.

He said softly: "This is it, Karen. Tell the monk that the jeep will go once I have fitted these last few parts, but tell him also that I can't see to finish the job until daylight. We must spend the night here."

Karen nodded and rose to her feet. Her white overall was smudged with black grease now, and so was the dark gold of her face. She was apprehensive but she crossed the courtyard and spoke to the monk.

Mason watched as he packed his tools into their box and covered the remaining parts of the engine with a clean sack. His heart was pounding just a little faster than usual, and he knew that he was taking a grave risk by forcing himself into the monastery for the night, but outwardly he was calm. He saw a second robed figure join the first facing Karen, and moved up beside her, smiling, and shrugging his shoulders helplessly.

The monks were angry but again they were led inside, this time to a larger, better-lit room, where five-coloured prayer flags adorned the walls and there were cushions and silk curtains to relieve the bareness. More food was provided, goat's cheese and bread, and more of the greasy butter-tea.

As they ate Karen said quietly: "Several of these monks I know from my previous visits, but they refuse to recognize me." She looked at him levelly and said unashamedly: "I am scared, Paul."

He smiled. "So am I, but somehow I don't think they dare murder us on their home ground. Did you manage to tell them that I left a message for Lieutenant Sangh to tell him that we are here?"

She nodded. "I was able to mention it, and I have a feeling that that is the only thing that keeps us alive. They know that if we do not return the army will have to come up here and look for us. But it is unwise to try their patience too far."

"Don't worry. I won't do anything more to antagonize them."

They ate in silence after that, for Mason's brain was again searching for some way of making use of the slight advantage they had won. They were inside the monastery for the night, but at the moment three guardian monks watched over them and he still knew no more than when he had started out from

Tagantse. He had searched the face of every monk he had seen since his arrival, but he had not found one to match the size of the frightening ape-like man who had attacked him in his billet.

The problem was unexpectedly taken out of his hands when yet another monk, an older man this time with a deeply-lined face, appeared in the room. He entered silently and startled both Mason and Karen when he started to speak.

The monk who had first met them, and who seemed to be responsible for them, arose to listen to the old man's words. He evidently disagreed, but the old man carried some authority that overruled the protest. Karen listened to the exchange and Mason saw a hopeful look flicker into her soft olive eyes. She turned to him excitedly.

"Paul, we're in luck. The old Abbot wants to see us. I thought that the rumours must have been right and that he must be dead when the sour one refused to let me see him when we first arrived. But now it seems that he's sent for us of his own free will."

The monks were still quarrelling and she quickly waved her hand to stop his answer as she strained to understand what they said. Mason watched the faces of their hosts, their expressions made doubly sinister by the smoky shadows from the lamps and the vehemence of their own agitation, and felt a ripple of excitement as he realized that the new arrival was standing firm. The sour monk, their original host, finally had to give way and turned sullenly to speak to Karen.

When he had finished she smiled at Mason.

"We have to follow the old monk. He will take us to the Abbot." There was a flush of relief in her face and she added happily: "All this mystery will be cleared up now. I know it will."

Mason was not so sure, but he smiled as though he were as he helped her to her feet. The old monk made a commanding gesture and they followed him as he left the room. The sour monk and one of his companions fell into step behind them.

The route twisted and turned through

178

a maze of smoky passage-ways, lit only by the flickering lamps and lined with the inevitable statuettes and prayer flags. Mason made an effort to keep track of the many changes of direction, but very soon had to admit that he was lost. He guessed from the size of the place that many more monks must have once lived here than the thirty that Karen had estimated from her last visit. Several times they saw more of the orange-robed men moving like bright but fleeting ghosts in the branching passage-ways, but none came close. Finally they halted before a closed door where two of the larger monks stood guard.

The old monk who was their guide spoke to the guards and the door was opened. The old man went inside and they heard him speak in reverent tones. A moment later he returned and bowed them inside.

Mason had not been sure how to visualize the religious ruler of this strange, vast household, and so he entered with an open mind. Karen was positively eager beside him. They were both disappointed for the room was empty. All four walls were hung with heavy velvet curtains, to the left and right and around the doorway they were dark blood red, but directly ahead they were gold. A tall pedestal with burning incense stood in each corner, and more flickering lamps gave off a smoky light.

Mason felt Karen press closer against him as they stood in the centre of the room. The four guardian monks filed inside and paired off to left and right with their backs to the red drapes. The old monk stood behind them. Mason looked round, expecting the unseen Abbot to make his entrance through the door behind the old monk's back, and then a voice greeted them from behind the golden curtains.

"Captain Mason — Doctor Langford — why do you come here?"

Mason faced the sound, aware at the same time that the door had silently closed behind him. Karen answered for him.

"We came to help one of your brothers whom we were told had broken a leg.

Now our vehicle has broken down and we cannot leave."

"Perhaps I could believe *you*. But why does Captain Mason come? What does a British officer want at holy Karakhor?"

Mason stared at the golden curtains. Karen had gone rigid beside him and the cold wriggling sensation was again chilling the back of his neck. The hidden voice was squeaky, like the unbroken voice of a boy child, except that no child could have spoken with such savage intensity. The wriggling, like the frozen belly of a snake, travelled slowly down Mason's spine, and with an effort he forced himself to answer.

"I came because it is not safe for a woman to drive alone through this violent country. The man who usually drives her jeep was killed a few days ago and she has not been able to find a replacement."

"And that is all?" The squeaky voice was sarcastic.

"Not quite." Mason hesitated, knowing that he was on very dangerous ground. "There are strange rumours in the villages about Karakhor. The people say that the Abbot is dead."

"But I am the Abbot. I am alive."

Mason swallowed hard, recognizing the note of hysteria in the hidden voice. He knew that he had almost gone too far.

Then Karen said suddenly:

"Your voice seems to have changed since last we talked. And why do you hide behind those curtains." She started to move forwards and instantly the stout wooden staff held by one of the monks who had guarded the door was thrust across her chest to hold her back.

"Stop!" the hidden Abbot commanded sharply. "The illness that changed my voice has also changed my face. No one must approach these curtains."

Despite the staff that the alert monk extended unyieldingly across her breasts, Karen's expression became suddenly hopeful.

"But I am a doctor," she said earnestly. "If you have been ill perhaps I can help you. If you will only — "

"No! No one can help me."

"But perhaps I can. You know

me — you must remember me. Surely you can trust me?"

"No. No one must see me." The squeaky voice became dangerous in its agitation, the pitch rising in volume. "You are not wanted here do you understand? We are capable of taking care of our own sick, we do not need your help. Holy Karakhor is a place of meditation and prayer, we do not want unbelievers who do not follow the true path of Buddha. We wish only to be left in peace to pray. We wish only — "

The unseen voice raved on, wavering from its first unearthly squeaking to a high pitch that was almost a shrilling scream. The words were a combination of religious wanderings and mingled, scarcely veiled threats, but it was the voice itself that struck home with the most effect. Mason suddenly recalled Radhaven's phrase, *a mind of evil*, and realized that here was a voice that fitted the same word. There was no other way to describe it. The voice behind the curtain was the most evil distortion of human speech that he had ever heard.

Karen was trembling slightly beside him, but outwardly her thinly beautiful face was palely calm in the smoky light. The attendant monk still held the barrier of his staff across her breasts, but she kept her arms at her sides. Mason could still feel the crawling sensation down his spine and his fingers craved to touch the revolver at his hip. He had the feeling that at any moment he might be forced into a suicide effort to shoot his way out, and knew that in this dark rabbit warren of passages he had no hope whatever.

"You, Captain Mason." The voice shrilled his name to command his attention. "You are far from your homeland, and you interfere in matters that do not concern you. You follow a dark and dangerous path and ignore the signs of warning. My meditations bring me many visions, and for you I see only deeper darkness and death. Tonight you may sleep well, for tonight you rest safe in holy Karakhor. But once you leave — "

The voice trailed into silence, and Mason, stiffening under the naked threat, had to kill the urge to spring forward and tear open the golden curtains. Then the hidden Abbot spoke again, and his voice had lowered to its first squeaking tone.

"I am tired. The audience is at an end. Tomorrow you will both leave, and you will not return again to holy Karakhor."

There was no more sound from the closed curtains, and after a moment the old monk behind them spoke an order. The guardian monk who still held his staff at right angles immediately pressed Karen back. Mason took her arm and they both turned to leave. There were a thousand questions that Mason wanted to ask the now silent voice, but he knew that he would receive no answers. He had been warned, and that was the sole purpose of the audience.

They returned to the passage-way, and as the door closed behind them on the curtained room, Karen pressed close against his side. There was a tremble in her body again, and he saw that her face was tense and frightened.

She whispered hoarsely: "Paul, that wasn't the Abbot. I'm sure of it. Even if his voice could have changed through

185

an illness, the old Abbot didn't speak a word of English!"

Mason held her arm more firmly. "He may not be the same Abbot whom you knew," he said softly. "But our mysterious friend with the sickly voice is most certainly the Abbot now. The question is, what happened to the first one?"

11

A Prowl by Night

The old monk with the lined face was again in the lead as they were escorted away from the audience room. The two monks with their heavy staffs had resumed their sentry positions outside the door, but Mason could hear the soft footfalls of their original two guardians close at their heels. Karen was still trembling a little beside him, her fear very real now that she knew she no longer had a friend in the Abbot, and that the old Abbot was most probably dead. They reached a T junction at the end of the dim-lit passage, and Mason felt a stab of apprehension as the old monk turned left instead of right, leading them not back towards the courtyard but deeper into the monastery.

The old monk looked round and spoke briefly to Karen as they turned the corner behind him, and Mason saw the quick jump of alarm come into her eyes.

"What's wrong?" he asked softly.

The old monk was striding forwards again with his back towards them and Karen turned her face to Mason as they followed, her eyes were still scared.

"He said our rooms where we can spend the night are this way. Rooms, Paul, not just one room. They're going to separate us!"

Mason swore softly, his jaw tightening. He had not expected this, and yet he knew that he should have done. This was a monastery where men lived chaste and sexless lives, and even in ordinary circumstances the monks would not allow a man and a woman to share the same room. Without provoking trouble there was no way they could avoid separation and he knew it. He knew too that it could prove fatal to let Karen out of his sight, and that at the very least it would be condemning her to a sleepless night of lonely fear.

At last he murmured grimly: "We'll

have to accept it, Karen. I'm sorry, but we don't have much choice."

He glanced up to make sure that the old monk's back was still towards them, and then reached carefully for the revolver at his right hip. He pulled Karen close so that their bodies were touching and shielding the movement of his left hand from the two monks behind. The bad, smoky light of the passage-way was an added advantage as he pulled the revolver from its holster and passed it in front of their bodies.

"Here," he said quietly. "You'd better take this. I don't think you'll need it, but it will make you feel safer."

She hesitated. "You might need it more than me."

"Don't argue."

At any second the old monk could become suspicious of their whisperings and glance round, and so he pushed the revolver into a gap between the buttons down the front of her overall. She clutched it with both hands, and then swiftly pulled the overall open and stuffed the revolver inside. She fastened the buttons again with unsteady fingers.

"I still think you should have kept it," she said worriedly. "They tried to kill you before in your own billet. You'll be in more danger here."

"I don't think so," he reassured her. "If last night's attempt had succeeded it would have been murder by persons unknown, but if I'm killed here they can't fail to implicate themselves. Besides, the new Abbot wouldn't have bothered with trying to warn me off if he means to have me murdered immediately afterwards. There'd be no point."

They turned another corner, and traversed yet another narrow passageway, and then at last the old monk stopped in front of a closed wooden door. He pushed it open and turned to bow Karen into the small barren cell inside. The room was lit by moonlight from a square window cut out of the wall, and contained a low palliasse, some rush matting and a crude chair.

Karen hesitated unwillingly before the doorway, glancing helplessly at Mason. The old monk sensed what was disturbing her and his expression became unexpectedly kindly. He turned and gestured reassuringly to the next door down the passage to indicate that Mason would not be too far away.

Mason said quietly: "Don't worry, Karen. I'll be within hearing."

She nodded and then went inside. The old monk spoke to her for a moment, and then he closed the door behind her. He moved on and Mason followed him to the next room, aware all the time of the two guardian monks trailing silently behind. The old monk pulled open the door to reveal another bare-walled cell, identical to Karen's, and then waved the Intelligence man inside.

As the door closed behind him Mason pressed his back against it and listened with his ear close to the rough wood. He clearly heard the sound of muttered voices, and then the swish of robes retreating along the passage. There was no more sound, but he was sure that only one man, most certainly the old monk, had left. The two guardian monks were still there. He guessed that they would

191

stay all night outside his door, perhaps taking it in turns to sleep across the threshold.

Slowly he examined his cell-like room. The stone walls, floor and ceiling were solid. There was only the straw palliasse and a crude chair, splashed with moonlight from the open space of the window. He turned to the door; there were no peepholes, but there was no lock or bolt and no way to bar it. Finally he went over to the window.

He had been faintly surprised to find an alternative means of exit, but when he looked down he saw that there was no way out from here. Below the window was a hideous drop to the bottom of a thousand foot gorge where jagged rocks glinted dully in the faint starlight. The dizzy sight was strangely, terribly beautiful, the great drop contrasted by the mighty peaks rising far to his right in magnificent towers of snow and ice against a light-pricked canvas of night sky.

He smiled grimly as he realized how neatly he was trapped. On one side the sheer drop, and on the other the whole impossible maze of the monastery.

For a moment he simply stared, and absorbed the dark sweep of the gorge into his mind. Even in his present position the view could not fail to command attention. Then his eyes became more purposeful and his gaze returned to the wall below him.

The wall was made of square blocks of rough grey stone, stretching down for twenty feet before reaching a narrow ledge that marked the start of the practically perpendicular rock face of the mountain shoulder on which Karakhor was built. There were more windows on either side, widely spaced, but on the same level as his own. The next window to his right was Karen's, but there was no sign of her. Above was another fifteen feet of blank stone before the eaves of the lowest roof level.

Mason studied the cracks between the stone blocks making up the wall for several long moments, and the idea they suggested made his stomach wince each time he looked down. Finally he turned back to face the door, his mind weighing the odds.

He made up his mind and dropped down on to the palliasse by the wall. The packed straw scratched and rustled underneath him and he was sure the sounds must be noticeable from the outside. He couldn't risk those rustlings when he arose in the night, and so he twisted as though making himself comfortable and rolled off the rough mattress on to the stone floor. There he lay facing the door, his eyes half closed but with no intentions of sleeping. He was conscious of the lack of weight at his right hip, and his stomach seemed as empty as the bare leather holster. He felt badly in need of a gun.

★ ★ ★

For three hours Mason lay on the stone floor, his body gradually growing stiff as the cold worked through him. He moved his muscles as much as he could to prevent them seizing with cramp, but dared not take the risk of making any noise. The huge monastery was totally wrapped in silence, and although at the start he had occasionally heard the shuffling of his guards outside the door, nothing had disturbed him for the past hour.

His mouth was dry as he checked the luminous dial of his watch and saw that it was time to move, for three hours was the limit he had set for waiting. The sentries outside had not once eased open the door to look in, and he felt sure that unless they were disturbed they would not think to check on him now that they had settled down. He had only to ensure that he both left and returned in absolute silence.

He pushed himself slowly from the floor, making no sound on the bare stone. He hesitated on one knee, crouching and listening, and then pushed himself upright with infinite care. His rubber-soled shoes were silent as he tip-toed around the palliasse and approached the window. Outside the grim drop looked more fearful than ever and his stomach winced again.

He stood for fifteen minutes, breathing

softly and massaging his wrists and ankles to ease out the stiffness of lying on the stone floor. There was still no interruption from outside and he tried to convince himself that the sentries must surely be dozing. They must be certain that the only way out was through the door, and, Mason told himself warningly, for any ordinary man with any sense they were undoubtedly right.

But the stiff training courses designed for field officers of Naval Intelligence, plus previous Marine Commando courses, turned a man into something more than ordinary. And Mason was well prepared for what he had to do tonight. There was a difference between his present task and scaling a sheer cliff face from a simulated assault beach, but the climbing principles and the necessary head for heights were the same.

He climbed silently on to the broad ledge of the window, and averted his eyes from the yawning emptiness below as he slid one leg outside and probed his toe into the horizontal crack between the cemented blocks of stone. Then, with one arm and leg still inside the window he inched his body outwards, his right hand groping above his head until his fingers hooked into another crack. Slowly he swung his left leg out of the window, feeling with the toe until it was firmly planted beside his right. Then he hung motionless for a moment, reassuring himself for the last time that no one had heard him leave, and then he left the window and began to inch his way sideways across that awful drop.

The cement used on the wall had been of poor sandy quality, and had crumbled away to leave deep cracks between the blocks on the sheer face, so that Mason was able to dig in deeply with fingers and toes as he worked his way across. His target was the next window to his right as he faced the wall, the opposite side to Karen's, and he had approximately fifteen feet to go. After the first yard his upstretched arms and the backs of his legs ached with the support of his full weight, and the harsh stone was drawing blood from his grazed fingers.

He moved carefully, but as fast as he

dared, knowing that if he took too long then he would tire and slip. It would only take one mistake to plunge him a thousand feet to his death and his face glistened with sweat. He knew better than to look down but nothing could wash the memory of those jagged rocks beneath him from his mind.

He reached the half-way mark, the point of no return, and his shoulders were dragging painfully at their sockets. There was a terrible temptation to pause, just for a moment, and rest. But he knew that there was no rest, only increasing weakness, and he forced his clinging body into continuing its fly-like progress across the wall.

The wind began to moan softly across the valley, plucking at his jacket with light, teasing puffs. He shivered and prayed that no stronger gusts came to flick him off into space. The next window was only an arm's length away now, but he felt so drained and weakened that he despaired of ever reaching it. The crack that his toes followed was becoming narrower, pushing them out until they barely gripped at all and he hung by his fingers alone. He made another six inches — another three — and then the fingers of his right hand slipped, the skin rasping away as they released him into the waiting abyss.

Desperately Mason thrust with his toes, pushing himself hard to the right as his flailing hand snatched for a grip inside the open window. His left hand slipped away and he twisted his body frantically as his feet dropped from beneath him. He fell less than a foot before his arms wrapped over the bottom edge of the window and jerked him to a halt.

He hung there helplessly, his chest heaving against the face of the wall, his legs dangling. His arms began to slip and then his fingers caught again on the inside edge of the window. He made a final effort to pull himself up and wriggled through the opening to slide face down on the floor.

He recovered his breath and stood up slowly, his knees still shaking violently. The room was another bare cell and fortunately it was empty, very fortunately, he thought, as he remembered the defenceless sprawl of his entry. He looked down at his skinned fingers and winced, and then moved slowly to the closed door.

There was no sound from the passage outside, and when he was sure that his breathing was steady and his nerves under control he gently eased the door open. Down the dim lit passageway to his left he could see the huddled orange robes of the two monks outside the room he had just left. Both of them were seated on the floor, cross-legged and with their heads bowed across arms folded over their chests. The movement of their breathing was deep and peaceful and he gathered courage for his next step, silently stepping out into the passageway and tentatively closing the door behind him.

A yard away was a branching passageway, and two soundless steps hid him from view of the sleeping monks. He froze with his back to the wall to make absolutely sure that the movement had not been noticed, and then proceeded warily along the passageway. He had no idea of what he expected to find, and could only prowl aimlessly and hope to stumble upon something that would help to solve the strange mysteries with which he was surrounded. Although he must not wander too aimlessly, or he would never find his way back.

The monastery was still shrouded in silence, like a veil drawn over something that is best not seen. The smoking lamps still gave their vague glimmers of light from the niches carved in the walls of the passageways, and the lines of ugly statuettes still watched with blind stone eyes. Mason had a vague impression of how to reach the audience room where he had received his blunt warning from the unseen voice of evil and now he trusted to his sense of direction to lead him back to it. He had to start somewhere.

He passed many closed doors, but caution forbade him to investigate behind them. He knew that he was taking a grave enough risk by prowling through the passages without stumbling into the cell of some restless monk and raising an uproar. He had to remember that if he was caught and the monks were provoked into violence, then Karen would suffer too. The monks most definitely could not allow her to return to Tagantse alone.

He followed faintly familiar twists and turns, taking care to ensure that each succeeding passageway was empty before he turned the corner, and at last he found the audience room again. This time there were no monks standing sentry outside, and he approached it warily. There was no sound from within, and ignoring the increased thumping of his heart he tried the door. It opened with no resistance.

Inside the lamps were still lit, and the incense still burned in the four corner pedestals. The curling smoke made dark, wispy patterns against the blood red drapes on either side. The room was empty.

Mason moved forward slowly, closing the door behind him. His memory was stark and clear and he could not suppress a shudder as he gazed at the golden curtains shielding the far end of the room. He swallowed hard and pulled the curtains to one side.

There was no one there.

For a moment Mason looked at the empty pile of silken cushions on which the Abbot had clearly rested, and then he saw a door in the wall beyond the recess. He moved towards it and listened. There was no sound, but when he tried the door it would not budge, and he dared not use force. He realized grimly that he was not going to get a glimpse of the new Abbot after all and allowed the golden curtains to fall back into place as he returned to the centre of the room.

For a moment he hesitated, but there was nothing to be learned here and he turned to leave. He moved back along the passageway the way he had come, knowing that if he strayed too far he would get lost. Then abruptly a door opened in front of him and he dodged sideways into a dark alcove behind a large statue of one of the deities, a grinning stone gorgon with a distended Buddha-like belly. He was only just in time.

A monk came out of the opened doorway, garbed in the usual long orange robe. He stared around slowly and

Mason's stomach tightened as he stared back from his place of concealment. The man's size matched that of his attacker of the previous night. Then slowly the monk turned and came closer along the passage. The smoky light showed up his thick, flabby features and broad, flaring nostrils. His head was shaven smooth, like the curve of a monstrous golf ball, and his eyes blinked repeatedly and with steady timing as he approached.

Mason pressed himself back into the stygian alcove, his heart pounding and the breath threatening to burst in his lungs as the large monk moved slowly past. And then he saw the ugly, very un-holy automatic gripped in the vast hairy fist.

The orange robes rustled menacingly as they trailed along the stone floor, and Mason watched as the ape-like monk reached the door of the audience room and pushed it open. The man stepped inside and there was a moment of silence before he reappeared. Then slowly he returned, again passing the darkened spot where Mason crouched. He stood for several moments outside the door from which he had first appeared, and then he slowly passed inside and drew it shut behind him.

Mason let the air seep out of his lungs and felt weak in the stomach at the narrowness of his escape. He was sure that he must have made some sound to alarm the man and suddenly knew that this mad venture was too dangerous to continue. He now knew without doubt that the assassins of last night had come from Karakhor, and with that he would have to be satisfied. He had to remember that he was not only risking his own life but the Doctor's as well.

He waited ten minutes to be sure that the armed monk was not trying to trap him into showing himself, and then moved out of his hiding place. He passed the closed door through which his enemy had vanished as swiftly as was silently possible, and then hurried back the way he had come. It took him ten minutes more to find the passageway where the two monks slept outside his own room, and he again crossed gingerly into the empty room from which he had started.

Again he had to make that terrifying crossing above the darkened gorge, and this time he started with the added disadvantage of already bruised and bleeding fingertips. But there was no other way. He forced himself to wait for several minutes and rest, then he climbed on to the window and swung his body once more into the night.

The return crossing was even worse than the first, for now the wind was stronger and blowing hard from the mountains. But this time there was one blessing in that he was able to cross the stretch where the toe-crack narrowed while he was still strong at the start, so that by the time his arms began to scream in agony and the muscles threatened to tear, he had reached the firmer line of the toe hold and could relieve the weight.

He looked down once at the thousand foot drop that opened like a hungry mouth to receive him, and his head swam with dizziness, and he knew that to do so again would be fatal. So he kept his face to the wall until the blessed moment when his left hand encountered his own window and he knew that he was home. He pulled himself inside and crawled on to his palliasse, careless now of the rustling of the straw and sobbing with relief.

12

The Second Warning

It took Mason several minutes to regain
his breath and his composure, but when
he had succeeded there was no sign that
the slight sounds he had made had been
heard, and nothing to indicate that his
nocturnal wanderings had been noticed.
He slowly regulated the harshness of
his breathing and killed the trembling
in the violently aching muscles of his
arms, and gradually he relaxed. For
a while he listened for any movement
from the monks outside his door, and
then he slept. There was nothing further
that he could achieve by remaining
awake, and he knew that any whisper
of danger, either noise or movement,
would penetrate his subconscious and
bring him instantly alert.

He slept lightly and restfully until
the first grey light of dawn began to

brighten his cell-like room. Beyond his window the sprawling outlines of the Himalayan peaks sharpened into brilliant focus and the sunlight glittered on the high wastes of snow and ice. The savage gorge absorbed the night shadows and its stony jaws reflected harshly in the daylight.

The shuffling noises as the sentry monks stirred in the passageway pinged gently on the radar of Mason's mind, and although he continued to lay in a sleeping position on his palliasse he became awake and waiting. Half an hour passed and then there was another movement outside the door, and the sound of low voices. Then the door was opened and the old monk with the lined face appeared.

Mason rose to his feet and smiled a greeting. The old man merely nodded and indicated that it was time to leave. He stood to one side and Mason passed out of the room beneath the hostile eyes of the two sentries.

They moved down the passageway and without ceremony the old monk pushed open the door of Karen's room.

She was standing by the window and wheeled round with alarm, her hand jumping nervously towards her waist, where Mason knew his revolver must still be tucked out of sight beneath her overall. Then she saw Mason and relief flowed into her sheepish smile.

They were led back through the gloomy passageways, avoiding the audience room of the Abbot and returning to the room where they had received their last meal the previous night. Here they were served with a frugal breakfast of flat, dry cakes, and more of the repulsive butter-tea. Afterwards they were escorted back to the courtyard. The old monk spoke sternly to Karen, and then fixed Mason with a sharp, warning stare before returning into the dark interior of the monastery. The sour-faced man who had first met them stayed on watch in the doorway with his companion.

Mason took Karen's arm as they moved out into the sunlight where their jeep waited in the centre of the courtyard. Her eyes were tired and strained, and he knew that she had slept little during the night, if at all. This was the first opportunity they had had to speak except for a brief exchange of greetings, and now she said quietly:

"Paul, the old monk insists that we leave Karakhor this morning. He says it is the holy Abbot's order." She paused, and then added: "I think they're almost certain that we're only fooling with the jeep."

Mason smiled as he removed the sack he had used to cover the scattered pieces of the engine.

"It doesn't matter," he said. "Because we were leaving anyway. I think we've learned as much as we can without bringing up a squad of troops to make a proper search. And I'll raise that question again with Radhaven the moment we get back."

She stared at him blankly. "But what have we learned?"

"Two things. One — the rumours were right and the old Abbot has been removed, even if he isn't dead. And two — the men who tried to kill me in my billet were definitely monks from Karakhor. I saw the big man who carried his friend to safety lurking around the passages last night with an automatic in his fist. Those two items should be enough to override Radhaven's objections, and if they're not then I'll go over his head and approach Samdar Rao."

Karen still stared, her lovely olive eyes slightly disbelieving. "But how, Paul? Where did you see this man?"

"Start fitting the carburettor together," he warned. "Our two guard dogs are giving us some dirty looks."

Karen spared a quick glance for the two orange-robed monks standing in the cloisters and then began to reassemble the pieces. Mason knelt beside her and gave her a short outline of his night's adventures as they worked. Her fingers slowed almost to a stop and her face paled as she listened.

"Paul, you fool. If you had slipped — "

"But I didn't slip," he interrupted firmly.

She looked into the calm blue of his eyes and her face was baffled. "I don't

212

understand you," she said slowly.

For a moment Mason did not comprehend either, and then he realized that she was attempting to reconcile a man who could cross that dizzy gorge with the gallant dandy who had kissed her hand a few nights ago. He smiled then, and said:

"You don't have to understand me, Karen. As long as you trust me."

She nodded slowly, her face regaining its colour. "You are a strange man, Paul. Almost two men. One careless and charming — the other hidden and very determined, almost frightening. But — " She answered his smile." — I think I trust you."

His smile became a grin, and then they concentrated on fitting the carburretor back on to the jeep's engine.

* * *

Half an hour later the job was done, despite the fact that Mason's skinned fingers hampered him badly and Karen had to do most of the work. They closed the bonnet and then Mason climbed behind the wheel. This time he turned the ignition key and contrived a pleased expression at the success of his repairs as the engine burst merrily into life at the first tug on the starter. He left the engine running as he dismounted to pack up his tools, and out of the corner of his eye he saw the sour-faced monk leave the cloisters and come out into the sunlight towards them.

Karen moved to meet the monk and they exchanged words as Mason lifted the tool box into the back of the jeep. The monk's tone was polite but commanding, and then it became softer and a note of menace crept through the politeness. Mason felt faintly uneasy as he listened and moved to Karen's side. The monk's eyes were cold in an expressionless face.

Karen answered the monk, and then glanced sideways at Mason.

"He says that now the jeep is repaired we must leave here immediately. It is now the time for meditation and prayers. He also says that we must take great care because our path is both narrow and dangerous. The monks of holy Karakhor will pray for our safety, but prayers cannot help those who ignore the signs."

Mason was tempted to smile at the second crude warning, but the humour died before it reached his face. He had to remember that he was not yet clear of the monastery, and even now the monks could stop him if they wished. And there was no doubt that both the unseen Abbot and the sour-faced man who faced him now meant their warnings to be taken seriously.

He said quietly: "Tell him that we're now going, and make a few appropriate thank you and good-bye noises."

She nodded and spoke more placating sentences. The monk accepted them gravely and with a slight inclination of his shaven head, and then he stepped back one pace. The gesture was both deliberate and final. Karen hesitated, and then Mason touched her arm and they both turned away and climbed into the jeep. Mason used the gears to turn the vehicle around in the courtyard and then drove out through the high wooden gates.

The monk watched them leave, standing piously with his hands crossed in front of him, and as they passed through the gateway Mason's eyes were fixed on the small motionless image in the glass square of his driving mirror. He saw a look of intense satisfaction cross the sour face, and then the orange-robed man turned slowly away to rejoin his waiting companion on the cloisters.

That maliciously confident expression scored in Mason's mind and caused a sudden, doubtful strumming along the more finely-tuned stretches of his nerves. Could there, he wondered, be any definite meaning behind those two badly-veiled warnings?

The question was just as abruptly forced out of his mind as the jeep's bonnet dipped sharply down the steep flank of the mountain's shoulder. Karakhor towered behind them, growing taller with every second, but Mason dared not look round as he concentrated on the dangerous descent to the valley. Karen sat equally tense beside him, her hands braced against the dashboard and her attention rivetted on the zigzag path that ultimately vanished into the tree-line below.

Mason kept the jeep in low gear and crept down gingerly with his foot hard on the brake. The sweeping view of the valley was magnificent, the trees filling the bottom like a dark green lake. On either side rose the slumbering ranges of the mountains, their rugged flanks bony with red and grey rock, rising to glistening winter white in the far heights to the north. The slope they descended was wild and stony, but relieved in places by golden pools of flowering orchids.

It took them twenty minutes to inch their way down to the dark line of the trees where the terrain levelled, and here Mason stopped to look up at the grey ramparts and golden roofs of the monastery. Then he looked at Karen and smiled.

"If there's ever a next time I think I'll leave the jeep round about here and walk up. I'm too young to let my hair turn grey."

Karen found a weak smile in return.

"The drive up was not so bad," she said. "But to drive down was frightening."

She stared up at the path they had followed, and then made an effort to push the memory out of her mind. She turned her face back to Mason and reached for his wrists to pull his hands away from the wheel.

"It is about time I looked at your fingers," she said. "We cannot be observed from the monastery now."

Mason nodded and turned his palms upwards to expose the grazed and torn skin of his finger-tips. They were sore and painful but he had refused to let her tend them under the eyes of the watching monks, taking no chances on arousing their suspicions. Now Karen winced as she saw the damage.

"Paul, they're almost raw!"

She examined them for a moment and then reached into the back of the jeep for her medical bag. Then it was Mason's turn to wince as she cleaned and dressed each finger in turn. Afterwards he asked her for the return of his revolver which he slipped back into its holster.

She watched him and said quietly: "Do you expect trouble, Paul?"

He smiled, and decided not to mention the parting expression he had seen on the sour monk's face.

"Not really," he said. "But in my job it's a habit to carry a gun. I feel lost without it."

She said no more and he put the jeep into gear again and drove on through the trees. After half a mile the track veered to the right and began to climb out of the valley once more, snaking up the flank of the main mountain mass and returning above the valley to Ladrung. Karakhor was again fully visible on its lofty perch, a stark, majestic outline that was gradually sealed from view as the road wound round the curve of the mountain.

Their conversation was limited by the endless jolting of the jeep and the fact that Mason could not let his mind wander too far from his driving. The sound of their engine was again advertising their presence noisily through the silence of the mountain air, but there was nothing that could be done about it except to stay alert. Then abruptly the jeep rounded a bend and there was a large boulder blocking their path.

Mason hit the brake pedal and the tyres howled as they skidded in the dirt. He stopped five yards from the boulder and saw instantly that there were no smaller stones or rubble as there would have been in a natural landslide, and there was no room to get past. He swore as he crashed the gear lever into reverse and jumped the car backwards, and as his left hand returned to the wheel so his right dived towards his holster. In the same moment the surrounding rocks became alive with rising, yellow-faced soldiers and a miniature arsenal of bristling machine-guns levelled towards them.

A shouted command, a burst of fire and Karen's scream all sounded at once, and the fast reversing jeep slewed sideways as the nearside back tyre was shredded by bullets. The jeep crashed backwards to a halt and then Karen threw herself on top of Mason and knocked the half-drawn revolver from his hand.

"No, Paul!" she begged again. "Please, no. They'll kill you."

Mason realized bitterly that she was right and that the odds were too hopeless for any resistance. The Chinese soldiers were closing around the crippled jeep and her swift action had prevented him from committing suicide against the dozen machine-guns aimed at his head. He swallowed hard and then switched off the roaring engine and very carefully extended his arms at full length towards the sky. Karen moved away from him and slowly raised her own hands.

For a moment Mason thought that they had had the ill luck to run into another far-ranging patrol scouting behind the Indian lines, but then he slowly realized that the grinning Chinese faces around him were far too confident for a reconnaissance party on enemy soil. They were relaxed and careless, supremely in command, and from their attitude Mason slowly saw the truth.

He knew now why the monks of Karakhor had been prepared to let them drive away, and why the sour-faced monk had smiled with such satisfaction at their retreating backs.

The Chinese Army had advanced silently during the night, surging across the valley and thrusting a spearhead between Tagantse and Karakhor. The troops had by-passed the monastery, ignoring it as unimportant as they advanced the battlefront to encircle the Indian Command Headquarters, but the movements had not been unnoticed by the watching monks from their lofty viewpoint. The holy men of Karakhor had known perfectly well that Mason could not fail to drive straight into the arms of the Chinese.

13

Prisoners of War

A Chinese Lieutenant approached Mason's side of the jeep, in his right hand he held a cocked revolver that pointed at the Intelligence man's head, and with his left he yanked open the jeep's door. Mason's revolver, which had lodged against the door, fell out on to the dirt track, and without looking down the Chinese kicked it calmly to one side. There was an ugly grin on the man's sallow face, but it was slowly replaced by a puzzled expression as he saw Mason's uniform.

For several moments they faced each other, and then the Chinese spoke haltingly in what Mason could now recognize as Hindi, the main Indian language. Karen answered him and there was a murmur of interest from the watching soldiers. The forest of slitted eyes regarded Mason with new interest, while those of the Lieutenant narrowed almost to extinction.

"So you are a British officer," he said flatly. "This is a strange discovery."

Karen said helplessly: "He recognized your uniform, Paul. I couldn't very well deny it."

The Chinese was studying Mason with the excited satisfaction of an amateur collector who has unexpectedly stumbled upon a very rare specimen indeed. Then he made a stiff bowing movement of his head and beamed.

"I am Lieutenant Sin Tai, of the Eighth Infantry Division of the Chinese Peoples Army."

He straightened up and waited.

"Captain Paul Mason, Royal Marines," Mason said slowly. "I am on a private mission not connected with the present differences between India and China. My companion is Doctor Karen Langford, a civilian. As non-combatants I must ask you to let us pass."

Sin Tai bared his teeth in a mirthless grin. "There are no non-combatants in this war, Captain. And in any case, you

224

are trespassing on Chinese soil. You are both prisoners of war."

"But this is India," Karen blurted angrily. "You have no right here."

Sin Tai said rudely: "This is China. The border line is due south of here."

"You know damned well the border is north — over twenty miles north," Karen cried furiously. "Your greedy land-grabbing claims are not recognized by anyone but yourselves. You — "

"Easy, Karen." Mason lowered one hand to grip her shoulder. "This isn't doing us any good."

Karen became silent, and the Chinese Lieutenant beamed again.

"That is very sensible. We Chinese do not wish to hear your foolish imperialist lies. The land belongs to Mother China, and we of the glorious Peoples Army will no longer leave it to the exploitation of India, the tame lap-dog of the west." He brandished his revolver suddenly and snapped: "Get down from the vehicle."

Mason obeyed carefully, keeping his hands well above his head. Karen hesitated and then shifted across the front seat and got out of the jeep to stand beside him. Sin Tai snapped another order and one of the soldiers instantly stepped forwards and ran his hands over Mason's body in search of hidden weapons. He found none and then looked from Karen to his officer. Sin Tai simply nodded.

Karen trembled and swallowed hard as the grinning Chinese soldier ran his hands lingeringly over her body. The man made a point of feeling around her hips and the inside of her legs, and she flushed faintly at the coarse chuckles and comments from those who watched. Mason's hands were balled into fists above his head, but his blood could only boil helplessly under the unwavering threat of a dozen machine-guns and the Lieutenant's revolver.

At last the soldier stepped reluctantly away from Karen and Sin Tai grinned approvingly.

"So you have no more weapons," he observed. "Very well, we will move down the track to a small peasant's hut I noticed before we heard the sound of your jeep. There you, Captain Mason, will tell me exactly what you are doing here in the Himalayas."

Mason had no time to protest, for the Lieutenant simply barked instructions to his men and turned away. The patrol of soldiers closed in eagerly and took a clear delight in jostling the two prisoners along the rough path.

They were pushed and prodded for two hundred yards before they reached a small, dilapidated hut of rough boards built against the mountainside a few yards from the track. A faded prayer flag hung limply from the top of a cairn of carefully stacked flat stones outside the hut's hanging door, and Mason guessed that it had been a resting place for pilgrims when pilgrims had been welcome at Karakhor. Sin Tai strode confidently inside, and Mason and Karen were pushed in behind him.

The inside of the hut was cramped, smelled of musty decay, and was flecked with splinters of light where the earth had fallen away from the chinks in the boards. It was empty but for a crude table of split logs, and on this Sin Tai seated himself arrogantly to face them, one toe just touching the bare earth floor. There was room for four armed men to stand guard behind Mason and Karen, while the remainder lounged outside.

The Chinese Lieutenant seemed to have emptied himself of any humour and regarded them coldly. "Now you will answer some questions," he said. His revolver jabbed Mason in the stomach. "You will tell me where your unit is stationed and how many troops the British have sent to join the cowardly army of India?"

Mason said flatly: "The last time I was on active service with my own unit was four years ago on an aircraft carrier in the South China sea. I don't know where she is now. And there are no British troops fighting in India."

Sin Tai slashed him calmly across the ribs with the barrel of his revolver. Mason gasped and staggered and Karen made an anguished move towards him that was stopped by one of the soldiers.

Sin Tai's yellow face beamed happily.

"Now you will tell me the truth. One officer does not come alone to a battle. How many British troops are in India?"

Mason breathed heavily, each breath paining him where the Lieutenant's blow had landed. He said slowly:

"I must repeat, Lieutenant, that there are no British troops in India. My presence here has nothing to do with the conflict between India and China. I am here on a special mission — "

"A special mission?" Sin Tai seized on the words. "You admit that you are a spy?"

Mason's teeth grated angrily. "No, damn you. I'm not a spy. Does a spy walk around in army uniform?"

"If there are no British troops and you are here alone then you must be a spy," the Chinese insisted. His slit eyes began to gleam and he burst out: "You are spying because the British troops are *coming* to India! That is the answer."

"It is not the answer — " Mason began. And then the Chinese swiped him viciously across the face with his revolver and knocked him sprawling to his hands and knees. He tried to rise and then Sin Tai's foot stamped hard on the back of his hand.

"You lie!" yelled the Chinese savagely. "The British are sending troops to India and you are here to spy in advance. You must tell me when these troops will arrive? Where they will be deployed? How many tanks and heavy guns they will bring with them?"

Mason looked up into the twisted yellow face and knew that nothing would convince this power-crazed fanatic that his own blinded opinion was not the truth. But he had to try. He had made up his mind on the way to the hut that his real enemies were not the Chinese but the monks of Karakhor, and that in his present position he had nothing to gain by concealing the true facts of his presence on the frontier.

He began as evenly as he could from his humbled position on the floor, but before he was half-way through Sin Tai kicked him coldly aside and snarled an order to two of his soldiers. There was nothing that Mason could do as the two men moved in with their clubbing rifle butts except to cover his face and stomach with his arms, and take the bulk of the blows on his back and shoulders. Karen screamed and put up a futile struggle that was checked by the quick stab of a gun muzzle in her ribs, and then she could only turn away sobbing.

When it was over Mason sprawled face down on the dirt floor, barely conscious. His battered body was a mass of burning pain and blood stuck his soiled shirt against his flesh in a dozen places. The beating had been finely calculated, and although the two soldiers had been careful to break no bones they had left the Intelligence man as helpless as a mound of pulped jelly. Sin Tai rolled the limp head from side to side with his toe and shook his head sadly. Then he turned to Karen.

"He should have told me the truth. It is a mistake to lie to a Chinese officer."

"But he did tell you the truth," Karen said desperately. "Or at least he tried to. He simply came here to trace some stolen arms."

231

Sin Tai eyed her speculatively, and then his hand shot forward and his fingers closed cruelly upon her cheek. His slit eyes shone with pleasure as he twisted the pinched flesh and saw the terror behind the tears in her eyes.

"It is an impossible story," he said. "But perhaps you can be persuaded to tell me the truth." He smiled, and then his gaze flickered down to the inert Mason once again. The smile became broader. "Or perhaps the brave Captain will speak first if we revive him and force him to watch."

He released her cheek and gave an order to one of his soldiers, then he reseated one hip on the rough table and waited. The soldier hurried outside and then returned almost immediately with a water bottle. With one foot he rolled Mason on to his back, and then he unscrewed the cap and shook water over the sickly white face.

Mason could feel the splashing and fought to stay in that dim, subconscious darkness away from the finer edges of pain. But like a rush of flame the aching agony was engulfing him again and he groaned and twisted as more water was sloshed into his eyes and nostrils. He coughed helplessly and when the water stopped falling he opened his eyes.

The Intelligence man was hoisted to his feet and held upright facing Sin Tai. Through a blurred haze he saw the sneering yellow face taunting him, and the man's words penetrated harshly into his mind.

"You are foolish, Captain Mason. But it is well known that even the stiff upper lips of the British can be made to tremble rather than watch the interrogation of a woman. Perhaps for the Doctor's sake you will talk. I will tell my men to strip her."

Mason's eyes cleared and anger brought a struggling return of strength to his body. The two men who supported him now held him back and his movement brought a sly grin to the watching Lieutenant.

"So it is true," he said. "The brave British do fear more for their women than for themselves." He turned his gaze towards Karen and spoke slowly

233

and deliberately to the remaining two soldiers.

Mason's face contorted and mad fury powered his frantic move to reach the grinning Lieutenant. Sin Tai's revolver raised for another restraining blow, and then Karen said sharply:

"No, Paul. Do not fight them any more." Her voice was calm as she looked into the wretched blue of his eyes. "Nakedness does not alarm me, Paul. I am a doctor and I have seen many naked bodies of both sexes. It does not shame or frighten me for others to see my own."

Mason hesitated, and for a moment even Sin Tai looked faintly surprised at her reaction. Then he lowered his raised revolver and said silkily:

"We shall see." And he nodded angrily to his soldiers.

Karen stiffened, and held herself rigidly as her overall was wrenched away from her shoulders, the buttons ripping in the eager hands of the grinning Chinese. Her eyes fixed on Mason.

"Nakedness is only a psychological

disadvantage, Paul. My clothes would not stop much of a beating."

Mason writhed inside and only the deadly snout of Sin Tai's revolver held him still. Despite himself he could not avoid watching as the soldiers pulled and tore the remaining clothes away from her unresisting body. Several times they almost dragged her off balance, but when they had finished and stood back her bearing was if anything more proud and regal than before.

There was silence except for the harsh, animal breathing of the soldiers. Sin Tai's eyes roamed admiringly over the smooth nude lines of her figure, lingering on the fine thrust of her breasts that stirred only slightly with her breathing, and then lowering over the shadowed muscles of her flat stomach to her closed thighs. Mason saw the flicker of rising interest in the Lieutenant's smiling face and his jaws locked together until they hurt as he held himself in check.

Sin Tai straightened up from the table, and although Karen's eyes registered distaste she did not flinch as he moved towards her. He reached out one hand and her skin crawled as he stroked the curve of her breast. The taunting slit eyes were boring into her own but mostly she was aware of Mason like a chained volcano only a few yards away and for his sake she suppressed a shudder.

Sin Tai turned back to meet Mason's glowering eyes.

"Well, Captain. What have you to tell me?"

Mason said desperately: "I've told you, I came to find some stolen arms. They were taken from a British Naval base in Singapore and it's my job to — "

He broke off as the Chinese Lieutenant turned calmly away. On one wall of the hut a few spindly branches from a bush outside had straggled through the cracks in the boards, and Sin Tai broke off the longest he could find. He came back with the springing twig in his hand and swished it sharply. Karen yelped and twisted painfully away as it cut across her left breast.

"The truth, Captain Mason," Sin Tai said casually. "Not the lies. The truth."

Mason struggled helplessly, held back by two men while the third rammed the warning muzzle of a machine-gun deep into his stomach. The fourth man had automatically gripped Karen's arms as she had attempted to turn away.

Sin Tai began to enjoy himself, flicking his evil little switch in quick, stinging blows at Karen's naked body. She twisted helplessly in the grip of the brawny soldier behind her but the Lieutenant's aim was sadistically accurate, each blow cutting across her thighs or stomach. Her eyes filled and overflowed with tears and then the switch scored on the sensitive nipple of her breast and forced another whimpering cry through her clenched lips.

Mason ceased his futile struggles and said savagely:

"One day I'll kill you for this — you stinking little Chink swine!"

Sin Tai turned with a hiss of anger and slashed him full across the face. Mason smiled through the blood that seeped from his cut cheek.

"Stinking Chink swine," he said again.

The word Chink seemed to goad the Chinese to fury, but his upraised arm trembled and stayed without delivering another blow. They faced each other, Mason bleeding but defiant, the yellow features of the Chinese contorting as he controlled his rage. Then slowly he lowered the switch.

"You seek to anger me, Captain," he snarled slowly. "To draw my attention from the woman. But you have failed."

He spun on his heel and strode back to Karen, smiling as she attempted to squirm away from him. He flicked the switch towards her and then checked it before it fell, a new gleam suddenly showing in his slitted eyes as he looked over her body. He turned then, slowly, and almost mincingly and beamed at Mason.

"Do you still refuse to tell me the truth?"

"You've already refused to listen to the truth," Mason said wearily.

Sin Tai smiled. "So you will not talk — not even for your woman. You have watched her stripped, and you have watched her beaten." The gleam came back into his eyes again and he finished softly: "Could you watch her raped?"

For a moment Mason's heart seemed to stop, the blood drained from his face and his body became rigid. He was devoid of all thought or feeling, and then Sin Tai chuckled happily and the sound brought life flooding back.

For the first time in his life Paul Mason was beyond the reach of his steel controlled mind, and all sanity washed away as his muscles surged with crazed power. His body whipped backwards, and then forwards again to tear free from his restraining guards. He kicked left to boot one man cruelly in the groin and lashed right with a sweeping blow that caught the second man full in the teeth and knocked him spinning away. Then in blind fury he launched himself at Sin Tai, his fist smashing towards the loathsome yellow face.

The blow never landed for the third soldier swung the barrel of his machine-gun to deflect it with a terrific crack that almost broke Mason's wrist. And then the butt of the weapon thudded into the pit of his stomach and brought him to his knees. Sin Tai's yell had already brought more men crowding into the hut and Mason was again secured.

The Chinese Lieutenant was hideous with rage and gibbered a flurry of orders. Two of the soldiers hurled Karen Langford on to the ground, kneeling on her arms to pin her shoulders to the dirt floor. Two more held Mason on his knees with his arms twisted savagely behind him. Mason was on the fringe of unconsciousness, but Karen threshed and kicked wildly. One of the soldiers grinned down at her lewdly and began to unbuckle his belt. Sin Tai grabbed Mason's hair, yanking his head hard back.

"Watch!" he raved. "Watch and never again attempt to strike a Chinese officer of the Peoples Army."

"The British troops," Mason gasped desperately. "They arrive on the twenty-fifth. Four divisions. Seventy-five tanks. All for the Tagantse sector." He gabbled frantic lies about planes, guns and field artillery, but Sin Tai was no longer interested.

"Watch!" the Chinese screamed again. "Watch and — " He stopped in mid-sentence, staring towards the doorway. Mason became slowly aware of the hush that had fallen over the hut and he too turned his eyes towards the door.

A second officer of the Chinese Peoples Army stood in the entrance, his eyes ranging distastefully over the scene. Mason recognized the rank tabs of a Major, and felt a flicker of hope as the man spoke curtly to Sin Tai.

The Lieutenant answered rapidly, respectfully, his arrogance fading almost to humility. The Major listened and then looked down at Karen.

"I saw a jeep on the track with a red cross painted upon it." His English was precise and careful. "It is yours?"

She had to swallow hard before she could answer. "Yes. I am a doctor."

The Major looked down at her for a moment and then waved the soldiers away. They stood up reluctantly and Mason was almost sick with relief as the

Major told her almost gently to rise and put on her clothes. He barked an order and Mason was also released, and all the soldiers filed reluctantly out of the hut.

Sin Tai made a nervous protest, but after another curt order he too left the hut. Only the new arrival was left.

Mason stood up weakly and clutched at the table for support.

"Thank you," he managed to say weakly. "I am very glad to see an officer of some superiority."

The Major nodded gravely. "It is fortunate that I saw your jeep, and the crowd of soldiers outside this hut. I am afraid that Lieutenant Sin Tai is somewhat crude and overeager in his methods. He also attempts tasks for which he is not qualified, and for that he will be reprimanded."

Mason forced a tight smile. "Thank you again."

The expression in the Major's eyes slowly killed Mason's smile, and then he said: "I think I should introduce myself. I am Major Kang Yat Su, and although I cannot condone the torture of a woman doctor, your presence here still requires a satisfactory explanation." He paused, then finished bluntly: "Let me add that my civilized principles do not extend to spies drawing a soldier's pay, and that if no explanation is forthcoming I am capable of more refined methods of interrogation than the clumsy Sin Tai. I shall not need to use the woman."

14

Desperate Action

There was silence in the small hut. Karen had stopped in the act of buttoning up her blouse, her face still white and her fingers trembling as she stared at the Major's back, and then over his shoulder at Mason's blood-streaked face. Mason was still having difficulty in holding himself upright, but his gaze remained level as he looked into the round, moonish face beneath the peaked military cap. The Major's expression was blank, but the dark eyes were sharp and hard in their narrow, wrinkled slits, and Mason saw that the threat was no idle boast. Kang Yat Su would be more ruthless than his Lieutenant if the need arose.

However, the Major also showed signs of more intelligence than Sin Tai, and he had already proved that he would not indulge in brutality for its own sake. The fact gave Mason a glimmer of hope. He had to cough to clear a racking pain from his chest, and then said:

"I have tried to explain to Lieutenant Sin Tai that my presence here has nothing to do with the border dispute between India and China. My job is to recover a consignment of stolen arms that have appeared in the area."

"But I heard you speak of troops and guns." The Major's tone was cold and flat. "While I stood in the doorway you were shouting of British troops due to arrive here in the Tagantse sector."

"That is true," Mason admitted. "But you saw the situation. I would have told any lie that came into my head, and those were the lies that your Lieutenant wished to hear. He was convinced that I could only be some kind of an advance spy for a large British force."

"And Lieutenant Sin Tai is wrong?"

Mason nodded weakly as his chest was racked by another fit of coughing.

Kang Yat Su's face showed neither belief nor scorn.

"Tell me more."

Mason drew a deep breath and then went into complete details. The Chinese listened carefully and without interruption, but his face remained uncompromisingly blank. Mason made his story as convincing as possible but at the same time his heart was sinking as he realized how impossible it sounded. The two glaring questions; how had the stolen arms reached Karakhor? and why should the holy monks use them to arm the simple villagers of Ladrung? were obvious holes in an unavoidably vague story. And without logical answers there was little hope that he would be believed.

Karen had moved close to Mason's side as he talked, her face was still pale and strained in the gloom, but she had re-donned her underclothes, slacks and blouse and her body was steadier. Her crumpled overall still lay in a heap on the dirt floor. The low mutter of voices came from the soldiers outside, but none of them risked the Major's wrath by appearing in the doorway.

Mason finished his explanations and still there was no change in Kang Yat Su's expression. He waited in the suddenly pregnant silence and felt Karen's hand on his arm.

Then Kang said bluntly: "You say that the first rifles you recovered were in the possession of Chinese soldiers, but no British arms have been purchased from any source by the Peoples Army."

Mason's stomach began to twist slowly and he prepared himself for another beating. He told himself bitterly that he should have stuck to the lies he had tried to tell Sin Tai. Kang watched him carefully for a moment and then turned to shout an order.

Mason braced himself and felt Karen pressing nervously against him as one of the Chinese soldiers appeared in the doorway. The Major rapped another order and the man turned away. Kang Yat Su returned his searching gaze to Mason's face and held it there until there was another movement in the doorway. A very young soldier entered holding a rifle in both hands.

Kang stepped aside and spoke curtly. The young Chinese instantly detached the magazine clip and handed him the rifle. Kang turned it for a moment, and then held the empty weapon out to Mason.

The Intelligence man accepted it, his eyes still on the Major's face. Then he looked down and despite his present position a tingle of professional excitement passed through him. The rifle was exactly the same as those that had been recovered at Ladrung. He twisted it to verify the serial number and then looked back at Kang Yat Su.

"This is one of the stolen rifles. How did your man get hold of it?"

The Major smiled faintly and reclaimed the rifle. He threw it lightly towards the youth and asked a few brief questions as the magazine was fitted back into place. The soldier answered hesitantly and was then dismissed. Kang turned back to Mason.

"He found the rifle on the battlefield ten days ago — exactly as you say the first three were found." He paused, and then fired another question. "You said that you questioned some Chinese prisoners and an officer at Tagantse — what was the name of that officer?"

"He was a Lieutenant — " Mason's mind groped back. " — Lieutenant Cheng Wu."

Kang smiled, and nodded approvingly. "The soldier you just saw was a member of Cheng Wu's unit before he was assigned as my orderly and driver. The men of that unit found half a dozen of those rifles discarded around a party of their comrades who had been ambushed and killed, after the sound of their approach had forced the attackers to take flight. This was just before that unit went into action at the front and Lieutenant Cheng and most of his men were taken prisoner."

Mason forgot the congealing blood on his face and back and shoulders as he stared into Kang's satisfied eyes. Beside him Karen too was losing her fear and taking a definite interest.

The Chinese Major went on calmly: "The report on that ambush was puzzling, partly because of the British weapons that were left behind, and partly because it was not an act that could be logically attributed to Indian troops, it was too far behind our own lines. I intended to question Lieutenant Cheng more closely, but of course that was impossible after he was captured. After that the more important issues of the war pushed the matter from my mind."

Mason said slowly: "So all the British weapons that have been found in Chinese hands can be traced back to Cheng Wu's unit, and were all picked up on the scene of an ambush. And if no Indian troops were responsible for that ambush then it can only lead back to Ladrung or Karakhor, the local people who would know enough about these hills and mountains to sneak through the battle lines without being detected. It all seems to fit the general pattern." He went on to explain the Indian Major Radhaven's views that some third party was deliberately provoking war on both Indians and Chinese to keep the border dispute at battle heat.

Kang Yat Su again listened with silent care, and then said: "Normally I would say that such a conclusion is crazy. There is no motive. But knowing that a proportion of the facts are true I am forced to believe what you say."

Mason's relief was almost painful, but he succeeded in mastering it and said hopefully:

"I think that on this one matter all our interests are on the same side, and consequently any help that you can give me will still be serving China. Can you suggest anything which might lead us to a possible motive?"

The Chinese smiled broadly. "You are quick to take advantage, Captain. But no — I cannot suggest anything. Except that the work must be that of a twisted mind."

Mason frowned, and then looked into the Major's face again. "But at least you appreciate that I am not working against Chinese interests. Can you grant Doctor Langford and myself a safe conduct through the Chinese lines so that I can continue my inquiries?"

The smile saddened on the moon-like yellow face.

"That is impossible, Captain. I believe your story, but even I have to answer to officers of higher rank. I am afraid that both you and the good Doctor must continue to consider yourselves as prisoners of war for some time at least. I cannot sanction your release without a much more detailed inquiry."

Mason felt thwarted, his previous relief sloughing away, but he knew it was no more than he should have expected. If their positions had been reversed he would undoubtedly play cautious and take the same line.

"I am sorry," Kang Yat Su said apologetically. "But this is a time of war, and such unpleasantness cannot be avoided. I will take you to our forward command post which is down in the valley. There, no doubt, there will be officers superior to myself who will wish to interrogate you."

Mason could only make a bitter, defeated motion of his head.

Kang turned away and walked to the door of the hut. He called to Lieutenant Sin Tai and they consulted briefly. Sin

Tai was clearly displeased, but equally clearly there was nothing he could do about it.

Karen said nervously: "What will happen to us, Paul?"

Mason tried to inject his smile with hope. "Nothing serious. At least the Major believes us, and he over-rules that sadistic little Lieutenant."

Karen nodded tamely, and then Kang Yat Su was beckoning them. Mason put his arm around her shoulders and led her forward. They blinked in the sunlight as they left the hut, aware of the disappointed faces of the soldiers who crowded around them, and of the furious eyes of Sin Tai. The Major led them through the crush to where his camouflage-patterned jeep was standing on the track. The boy soldier who had presented the British rifle was sitting stiffly behind the wheel.

Mason and Karen were ordered into the back of the jeep, while two of Sin Tai's soldiers faced them with levelled sten guns, each with one haunch propped on the jeep's side. Kang Yat Su climbed in carefully beside the driver, and after a last brief exchange of words with the watching Lieutenant he gave the order to drive off.

Mason could sense Sin Tai's eyes glowering at his back as the jeep lurched into motion, but the Lieutenant was no longer an important factor in his mind. Instead he saw only the evil steel noses of the two stens pointed at his head and he prayed that the bouncing of the jeep would not affect the reflexes of either trigger finger. Karen was pressing close against his hip and thigh but they did not attempt to speak.

The jeep rattled on around the curve of the mountain, and Mason sought grimly for some way of manœuvring an escape. He knew that despite Kang Yat Su believing his story, the Chinese would still assume that he must have learned something of the strength and forces of the Indian troops and that there would be more interrogations. The same was true for Karen, and the odds were that the next man to question them would be another sadist of the calibre of

Sin Tai. At the best they could expect only a long spell in a Chinese prison compound, at the worst more brutal torture and indignity. The only way out was to escape.

Mason kept his eyes downcast from the grinning faces of the two guards, attempting to appear as dejected as possible. At the same time his brain assessed the odds. The two guards could be easily overbalanced from their careless perches on the jeep's sides, but while the stens were fixed so unwaveringly at his head any attempt to unseat them would be sure suicide.

Desperately he dug into his memory in an effort to visualize every twist and turn in the track, his mind slowly unrolling the film of his drive out to Karakhor. He started at the point where they had left the Seral junction to turn on to the main track from Ladrung to the monastery. There had been another branching track there that descended to the valley, and he guessed that that was the route that Kang intended to take. Grimly his mind worked its way back, seeing the dirt road flowing again beneath the bonnet of his own jeep. His mind's eye groped around rocks, up steep climbs, through a narrow defile, and then with a flash of hope he remembered the miniature landslide where he had been forced to clear the way.

His mind decreased into careful slow motion. He remembered the fall of rocks that the sound of his engine had brought down as he drove through, and his sour thoughts as he realized that when he returned he would have to clear the path again. There had been a bend immediately after the landslide and if Kang's driver rounded that bend at the speed he was doing now then the jolt as he braked just might give Mason the chance he needed.

If the landslide was still there? He had to face the fact that with Chinese troops moving all over the hills and mountainside the landslide might have been properly cleared.

However, the thought provided a conceivable chance for escape, and it was the only one that Mason could see.

If the jeep braked sharply the guards would be jerked backwards, and the stens would be automatically deflected to the sky. Mason's muscles tensed and he prayed that the landslide was there. The risk would be great, but he had already determined that if the chance arose he would take it.

He kept his face downcast and his shoulders humbly bowed, but from the corner of his right eye he watched the flank of the mountain moving past as they circled above the valley. The guards were relaxed, slightly above and in front of him. He thought once of Karen as her thigh stirred against him, but then decided that he would rather see her dead from a chance burst of gunfire than mauled and raped by lusting Chinese soldiers.

He recognized the vital bend coming up and the moisture dried in his throat. The jeep's driver showed no sign of caution and it was sharply clear that either the fall had been cleared, or that the man was a stranger to the road and did not know it was there. Kang Yat

Su was equally unconcerned. The guards were still relaxed.

The jeep swept into the bend and the Chinese Major gave a yell of alarm. The landslide was still there, leaving only enough room to crawl through. The driver stabbed his foot frantically on the brake and the two guards were jerked backwards towards the front seat. For a single second the stens were pointing skywards as the two men fumbled to retain their balance, but in that second Paul Mason exploded into desperate action.

His body thrust forwards beneath the two sten guns and lunged upwards with every ounce of tensed-up power. His right fist crashed out like a spring-loaded piston to crack home beneath one guard's jaw and send him flying backwards out of the jeep. His left hand clamped on the second man's sten and forced the barrel even farther upwards and then that murderous right swept across the front of his body, his shoulder fully behind it as it connected against the cheekbone. The bone crunched and Mason tore the sten gun clear of the man's hands as he somersaulted head over heels to join his battered companion on the track.

Kang Yat Su had twisted in his seat, his hand clawing for his revolver, and then Karen had thrown her arms around him from behind. The jeep skidded to a stop and without hesitation Mason slammed the driver unconscious with a quick blow of his newly acquired sten. The Major became instantly still as the sten's cold eye nuzzled his cheek.

Mason glanced back swiftly to the two guards sprawling behind them. The man with the broken cheekbone was whimpering helplessly, lying on his side with both hands pressed to his face. His companion was winded and making no attempt to reach his fallen sten which had landed a few yards away.

He said breathlessly: "Pick up that second sten, Karen, and take the Major's revolver."

Karen nodded, almost in a daze, and then she scrambled out to collect the sten. She ran back to the jeep and relieved the Major of his revolver without meeting his eyes. Then she stood back and waited.

Mason slowly removed the sten from Kang's cheek.

The Major said savagely: "You cannot get away with this, Captain Mason. You will never get through the Chinese lines. This road is blocked off by a strong detachment of infantry at the crossroads to Seral and Ladrung, and the valley below is thick with Chinese troops."

Mason forced a brief smile. "You don't know the British, Major. We have a national weakness for what's known as *having a go!* Which means that we'll try anything once."

15

Through the Chinese Lines

Lieutenant Panjit Sangh stood outside the India Command Headquarters at Tagantse, his handsome face grim as he stared into the gathering dusk where the deep *crump! crump!* of the Chinese artillery was now dangerously close. Tagantse was virtually surrounded on three sides and at any moment the signal could come for complete evacuation. At the moment the Chinese advance had halted while their heavy guns softened the resistance ahead, but the silence of the big guns would mean that the yellow soldiers of the steamrollering Peoples Army would again swarm forwards through the hills. It would be the fiercest battle yet.

Slowly Panjit Sangh walked towards his jeep. In his breast pocket was the note he had found in Mason's billet the previous day, informing him simply that

Mason and Karen Langford had driven to Karakhor. He was certain that their continued absence could only mean that they had been caught up in the surprise Chinese advance, but he was still torn between conflicting senses of duty. On the face of it there was nothing that he could do to help Mason, and when the battle started he would be needed in the defence of Tagantse. Yet at the same time he had not been re-assigned to his unit and he was still technically Mason's aide, which meant that he was the officer responsible for the Britisher's safety.

He reached the jeep and stood with both hands on the door, his mind silently worrying at the confliction of loyalties. Then slowly he decided to compromise. If the Chinese followed their normal pattern the artillery would continue the softening up process for another two or three hours yet before the infantry assault began. He would use that period of time in driving out to Ladrung, which was still just within the Indian perimeter, and attempt to learn the Chinese strength on the Karakhor road. If it was impossible to go any farther, or to learn anything of Mason from the villagers, then he would have done everything in his power and would return to Tagantse.

He yanked open the door of the jeep and swung his slim body nimbly behind the wheel, his confidence returning now that the decision was made. He paused only to unsnap the flap of his holster so that the revolver could be swiftly drawn if necessary, and then he started the engine. Deftly he crashed through the gears, reversing the jeep and swinging round to face the Ladrung road. Then he stamped his foot hard down on the accelerator and drove off as fast as was possible without killing any of the hurrying Sikh troops passing through Tagantse on their way to the front.

It was already dark as he reached the open road and raced through the troubled night towards Ladrung.

★ ★ ★

It was also dark in the narrow crack in the rocky mountainside where Paul Mason and Karen Langford had hidden in acute discomfort throughout the long afternoon. They were both cold and hungry, and their bodies still ached and smarted from the beatings they had received, but at least they were alive and free.

After their successful escape attempt Mason had wasted no time in securing Kang Yat Su and his three men while Karen held one of the captured stens. He had lashed their wrists and ankles together with a combination of bootlaces and belts, gagged them securely with strips from their own shirts, and dumped all four out of sight from the road. Then with Karen beside him he had driven on in the jeep.

He had driven as close as he dared to the crossroads where Kang had clumsily warned him that he could expect to find more Chinese troops, and then he had turned it off the track behind a mound of boulders. A poor hiding place but the best he could find. Here he selected one of the sten guns and slipped the Major's revolver into his own holster. He also took two full water bottles he had retrieved from the two guards and an excellent pair of binoculars that he found in a leather case in the front of the jeep. Then he had smiled warmly at Karen and led her diagonally up the mountainside until they had reached their present refuge to await the coming of night.

Throughout the long, nerve-wracking hours of daylight he had watched the road and the valley below through the stolen binoculars, which he found to be as powerfully effective as any British make. The valley swarmed with troops but not until late afternoon was there any activity on the road to indicate that Kang Yat Su and his men had been discovered and released. Mason watched a strong detachment of armed men searching along the dusty track and the lower slopes of the mountain, and prayed that none of their officers would think to search above the road. Behind him the sheer sides of the mountain were unclimbable without the proper equipment of ropes and spikes, and when the time came for him to come out of hiding the only way was down. He had backed himself into a dead end knowing that he could not survive on the lower slopes or in the valley in daylight, but if the Chinese were sharp enough to anticipate his movements his present chances were equally nil.

Karen crouched beside him and from time to time he gave her the glasses so that she could see for herself the situation they faced. The prospect of descending to the valley and attempting to penetrate the Chinese lines made her face pale, but she made no comment and instead talked quietly of other things. Occasionally she winced as her clothing rubbed and chafed at the cuts on her body, but as much as they could they both tried to ignore their physical pains.

The first crash of heavy shells shortly before dusk sliced through their struggling conversation and brought Mason scrambling to his observing position with the glasses to his eyes. He saw three distinct puffs of smoke along a ridge-top far along the valley towards Tagantse, and then another salvo sounded and more puff balls fountained upwards to dance and drift in the wind. Karen was close beside him and clinging tightly to his arm as he lowered the glasses and looked into her frightened eyes.

"It looks like they're warming up for another battle," he said slowly. "Probably an all out thrust against Tagantse this time. We'll have to leave as soon as it's dark enough to cover our movements, otherwise we might leave it too late. I should hate to get back to Tagantse and find that we're still behind the Chinese lines."

Karen flinched at the sound of another barrage of distant explosions. "Can we get through that?" she asked.

Mason's face was grim. "We'll run the risk of getting blown to pieces," he admitted. "But at the same time everybody else will be keeping their heads down so there's less chance of being spotted and shot up by the Chinese. All in all the odds against us are not much higher."

Karen nodded dully and closed her eyes. Mason hesitated, and then put

one arm around her shoulders and held
her close.

"We'll make it," he said. "Don't
worry." And he wished that he could
believe it.

* * *

The sound of the distant shells were still
exploding through the darkness when
Mason at last stood upright and helped
Karen stiffly to her feet. The sounds of
the search had long ago stopped on the
road below and Mason was as certain
as he could be that the demands of
the approaching battle had called it off.
Mercifully the brilliant moonlight of last
night was blotted out by banks of cloud
and it was in almost pitch darkness that
they picked their way slowly down the
mountainside to the narrow track of
the road. Mason guided Karen with his
hand on her shoulder, his free right hand
gripping the sten in readiness.

Mason hesitated as he reached the
track, listening for a moment, and then
he dragged Karen swiftly across and

plunged down the rugged slope towards the valley a thousand feet below. He had mapped his course through the binoculars during the afternoon and now he moved as fast as he was able through the tangles of rocks and thorns that clothed the mountain's flank. Once clear of the road he had slung the sten over his shoulder and now he used his free hand to feel his way down. When he judged that he was half-way to the valley bottom he stopped descending and began to move east towards Tagantse. He was determined to stick to the mountainside for as long as possible.

For the next hour they worked their way above the Chinese positions in the valley. From above their own heads came the occasional sound of jeep engines and marching feet along the mule-track road, but there was no danger of colliding with a Chinese patrol here on the ruggedly steep flank of the mountain. The only real danger was the grave risk of missing their footing and crashing the remaining five hundred feet to the valley floor.

The clouds continued to provide a

thick blanket over the moon, but the darkness that was their greatest asset was at the same time their greatest enemy. Even in daylight their task would have been a risky undertaking, but now it was positively deadly. Once Karen slipped as they inched around a buttress of rock, and the whole weight of her body was thrown on to Mason's arm as she hung above the black pit of the valley. Mason was dragged to his knees but his fingers dug into a crack in the rock face and he held her. She struggled frantically to regain her footing and then they both crouched in trembling silence, afraid that her half strangled cry of fear had been heard. There was nothing more to alarm them and despite the racing agony of his own heart Mason gripped her arm firmly and led her forwards once more.

They were nearing the battle lines and the continued pounding of the Chinese artillery rolled like hellish thunder across the far mouth of the valley. The screaming whistle of the shells and the shuddering crump as they landed came so constantly now that Mason no longer cared about the occasional clink of his sten against the rocks, or the rattle of dislodged stones from beneath their feet. He doubted if any of their own slight noises could be heard above the racket below. Karen was breathing harshly behind him, and although he knew that she badly needed to rest he gave her no respite, knowing that they had to get through before the heavy stuff ceased its savage plastering and the main army surged forwards again. She stayed with him gamely and made no complaint.

Inevitably as they worked their way away from the main mass of the mountain they were forced down towards the valley floor. The road had twisted away above them continuing to follow the bend of the mountain towards Ladrung and was no longer within hearing. They were able to move faster now that there was no longer the danger of a fatal fall, but they both knew that now they had left the steep slope for more level ground they could at any moment walk straight into one of the Chinese positions. Once they heard voices and Mason instantly pulled Karen into a crouch, listening with thudding heart until the sound came again and then turning silently away from it. He had one arm around Karen's shoulders now instead of gripping her wrist, and he had again unslung his sten.

The crashing bedlam of the big guns was fast becoming deafening and the night was soiled with the stink of cordite and the swirls of evil smoke. Mason could feel Karen's body whimpering where she clung against him, and when he glanced at her thin, strained face in the gloom he saw the bright glisten of blood where she had bitten into her lower lip. But still she made no attempt to drag back. A dozen times in the next half-hour they had to crouch like frightened animals in whatever concealment they could find to dodge the noisily moving patrols that hurried past with clinking arms and scraping boots, and only the fact that the enemy were confident and making no attempt to maintain silence enabled them to avoid the positions of the troops already dug in.

The terrain was mostly jumbled foothills,

scattered boulders and small trees, but it was the darkness that provided their best cover. The crack and recoil of the big guns were slowly shifting behind them, but the more frightening roar of the shell bursts were still ahead and Mason knew that they were slap in the middle of the Chinese lines.

He pulled Karen up the slope of a low hill and his heart almost tore up through his throat as he heard a crisp command in Chinese from the opposite side of the crest. He dived for a clump of rocks, stretching flat and hugging Karen close beside him only seconds before the speaker appeared over the rise. It seemed impossible that they had not been heard as Mason crushed Karen to the ground and buried his own face in the dirt, but the man's feet scraped hurriedly by without a pause. A Chinese patrol of eight men scrambled after their leader and passed in single file within three feet of the two fugitives as they trotted on down the slope.

Mason lifted his head and eased the breath from his frozen lungs as the last man vanished into darkness and felt Karen begin to sob painfully for air beside him. He could feel the terror in her shaking limbs and for a moment he forgot his sten as he gripped her shoulders and brought her face close to his own.

"Don't give up now, Karen," he whispered desperately. "We've come too far to turn back. We must be almost through."

"I'm scared, Paul." Her mouth quivered uncontrollably as the words trickled out. "I'm so terribly scared."

"Of course you are," he said gently. "So am I. I'm sick scared. And so is every other living soul near enough to this blasted battlefield to get killed tonight."

He took her hand suddenly and pushed the trembling fingers inside his tunic, pressing her palm to his left breast.

"Feel," he told her. "My heart's thudding even faster than yours. But we've got to control it, Karen. There's no shame in fear, but you have to control it."

He smiled at her as they knelt facing

each other in the dirt, and then slowly she forced a feeble smile in return and nodded.

"I'll try, Paul. I promise you I'll try."

He smiled again and impulsively embraced and kissed her, tasting the blood from her bitten lip as she shuddered against him.

"That's to take your mind off the present," he said. "Because there's going to be more to come after I've got you out of this."

She breathed deeply. "It's all right, Paul. I'm ready now."

He nodded as he picked up his sten, and then he helped her to her feet and they hurried on over the crest of the low hill.

They moved with absolute caution now as Mason strained every sense into the night-shrouded violence around them. His eyes ached as he concentrated his stare in an effort to pierce the blackness ahead and his ears strained to pick out the sounds of immediate danger from the overall bombardment of booming artillery. The shells were bursting directly ahead now and he knew that they must be exploding among the Indian positions. If only they could get through that final barrier of flying shrapnel and mushrooming dirt they would be safe.

And then he heard a rustle of movement to his left and again he was dropping flat on his stomach and pulling the stumbling Karen down with him. The rustle was repeated and then there was another sound from his right. A voice muttered from the veiling blackness and there was a clink of steel on stone. A cold wave washed over him as he realized that the Chinese were all around him. For a moment he lay as though petrified, and then he realized that he still had to go forward. He inched his head closer to Karen and pressed his mouth against her ear.

"Crawl," he whispered softly. "As silently as you can."

He sensed her slight nod of acknowledgement, and together they began to worm their way forwards. After the first few inches Mason gritted his teeth and reluctantly left his sten behind. The ground was too stony and he knew that only silence could help them now. The sten made crawling awkward and could easily clink against a rock. He still had the revolver in his holster and would have to rely on that. If they were heard they were finished anyway for he sensed that there were far too many Chinese around him for either weapon to save them.

The next twenty minutes were a long drawn nightmare of crawling and wriggling through the hell of war-torn darkness. Hard stones and jagged rocks struck at their bodies as they pressed forward, and a dozen times Mason was forced to grip Karen's arm and change her direction as they almost blundered into a Chinese fox-hole. They progressed like blind, groping snakes as their ears guided them through what had to be the most advanced positions of the Chinese lines.

Then abruptly a shell landed less than fifty yards to their left, the sound hammering through their eardrums as shrapnel whistled overhead and clods of earth sailed all around them. A second shell hit even closer and Karen screamed as the impact shook the earth beneath therm. Mason's arms encircled her head instantly, partly to shut off the scream as he crushed her face to his chest but mostly to protect her from the falling rain of soil and rocks that clattered around his shoulders.

"Paul, I can't — " she sobbed helplessly. "I can't go any farther."

"This is almost the end," he hissed urgently. "We must be through the Chinese. They wouldn't shell their own men. Come on now."

He rose to his knees, hauled her up beside him and began to dash blindly forwards through the night. Another shell blew up ahead of them and another crashed to their left and he automatically slammed her to the ground and sprawled on top of her as the disintegrating slivers of steel filled the air above them. Then he was up again, dragging her forwards. If he was fast enough he could get clear before the next barrage crashed down. But even as the thought spurred him on the chatter of a machine-gun suddenly filled the blackness with flashing flame behind him.

The first burst of tracer missed and he flung Karen again to the torn earth before the second burst sliced overhead, cursing bitterly as he realized that he had been heard by the Chinese. Karen writhed beneath him and he crushed a hand to her mouth.

"Keep still," he breathed in her ear. "Let them think they've scored a hit."

They lay in trembling silence for a moment, and then he whispered the order to crawl. Again they began to snake away on their stomachs and instantly the machine-gun blasted away behind them. In the same second another gun opened up ahead and Mason realized that his position had been pinned down by the Indian troops as well.

They were caught in the hell of no-man's-land between the two opposing armies, and both sides were taking no chances.

16

Disastrous News

Caught in the crossfire Paul Mason did the only thing possible as the two streams of bullets screamed through the darkness. He flung himself upon Karen's back and rolled them both over and over across the stony ground. Her choking cry of terror was crushed from her lungs as his arms locked round her and her legs flailed wildly as he desperately carried her sideways. The spitting bullets from the two machine-guns followed them blindly, chewing up the earth behind them as the gunners attempted to follow the sounds of their movements.

They were still tumbling over and over as the next bombardment of shells crashed down, the detonations creating a thunderous devil's tattoo upon the shuddering earth. In the drowning confusion of smoke and sound they were lost to the keen ears of the men manning the guns and the lines of spurting dirt that marked the raking bullets veered away from them. Simultaneously the ground ended beneath them and they crashed bodily down the slope of a still-smoking shell crater, tearing apart with the impact as they hit the bottom.

Bruised, battered and winded, Mason heard Karen choking and gasping close beside him and dragged himself towards her. Her body jumped at the touch of his hand but gradually became steady.

"Don't panic," he whispered hoarsely. "For the moment we're below the level of fire and both sides have lost track of us. We've got time to take a breather." As he spoke he prayed that artillery shells, like lightning, would never strike in the same place twice.

The final patter of falling dirt and stones gradually faded and silence crept like an alien threat through the smoke-filled night. Mason knew that both sides were listening for some sound to mark a target for their nerve-strung trigger fingers and could feel his heart-beat rushing like an express train inside his chest. Karen was equally tense beside him and he sensed the movement of her hand as she jammed it against her own mouth to muffle an unavoidable fit of coughing as the swirls of acrid smoke stung the back of her throat.

For a few moments they cringed face down on the moist, shell-torn earth, struggling to regain their wind yet at the same time hardly daring to breathe. Karen was trembling violently but her fear was under control. Mason fought to regulate his heart-beat towards normal and at the same time attempted to appraise their position. He judged that they were roughly three parts of the way across the separating stretch of no-man's-land, and much closer to the Indian lines than the Chinese. Their only hope was to identify themselves to the Indian troops and hope for covering fire while they made a run for the Indian positions, but the moment they shouted they would obviously draw a fusillade of gunfire from the Chinese at least.

However, there was no future in lying

in the middle and waiting for a lucky shell to blow them to shreds, and whatever the odds they had to take the only gamble there was. He wriggled closer to Karen until his lips pressed against her ear and said softly:

"You'll have to shout out to the Indians, Karen. Yell good and loud to identify us, but keep your head down. The moment you shout the lead will start to fly."

He sensed her nod in the thick gloom and they both pressed themselves as flat as possible against the earth. He heard her swallow hard as she moved her tongue to moisten her lips and then she half croaked and half shouted to the unseen troops.

Almost instantly the machine-guns flashed and rattled through the night and the dirt sprayed over their shoulders as the gunfire played around the edges of their shallow refuge. Karen shouted again, her voice tinged with hysteria, and abruptly both guns stopped.

Karen sobbed thankfully and struggled for breath, and then again she raised her voice, yelling frantically in Hindi in an effort to get the words out before they were drowned by renewed fire or shell bursts. Mason could picture the men of both sides listening as they crouched over their weapons in hidden foxholes, the Indians glancing at each other suspiciously as they recognized their own language, the Chinese hesitating only momentarily before squeezing off more shots at a confirmed enemy.

Perfectly in tune with Mason's thoughts the Chinese gun opened up again, its hateful chatter wiping out the rest of Karen's words. But the Indian guns remained silent, and here there was a flicker of hope.

The firing ceased abruptly again, and after a few minutes a cautious voice shouted from the Indian side. When the voice stopped Karen twisted to bring her face close to Mason.

"I've told them who we are, but they want to know what we're doing here," she said in exasperation.

"Blast them," Mason muttered angrily. "Just tell them that we were trapped by the Chinese advance last night. They can't expect us to give full details from here."

Karen nodded and shouted out the explanation, but before she could finish the Chinese machine-gun made another searching effort to locate her voice. More dirt splattered down across their shoulders but they were too low to be hit by the actual bullets.

There was a brief silence when the gun stopped, and then the cautious Indian voice hailed them again. This time the tone was slightly ashamed of itself, and Mason heard his own name mentioned in the inquiry.

Karen said grimly: "They want you to identify yourself and name your liaison officer in the Indian Army."

Mason gritted his teeth and shouted out his own name and that of Lieutenant Panjit Sangh. Then they both cowered from the inevitable reaction of the Chinese machine-gun.

The next silence was a long time coming, for the Chinese gunner was clearly infuriated for his failure to stop their shouting voices, but when it came the Indian voice fired out a rapid flurry of instructions and then there was more nerve-wracking waiting.

Karen whispered thankfully: "They're satisfied, Paul. The moment the next shells land they'll give us covering fire from both flanks. With luck we can reach their lines in the confusion."

Mason's jaw tightened at the thought, for despite this success the odds were still stacked against them. They had made contact with the Indians at the cost of confirming their position with deadly accuracy for the Chinese. And if any of the Chinese had understood the Indian instructions then the air above them would be alive with gunfire the moment the next salvo of shells hit down and they attempted to rise. Grimly he realized that now the most dangerous step still lay ahead, and that he and Karen would have to change their position before they could have any hope of making their last desperate dash for safety.

Mentally he blessed the courageous woman beside him for having the presence of mind not to acknowledge their instructions, for with luck the Chinese gunner might be fooled into thinking that they had not survived his last angry attack. Then his lips touched her ear once more, the dark hair brushing his cheek as he told her what they had to do. He felt the fresh shiver of fear run through her as he pressed against her side, but then it was controlled again and her head nodded in assent.

With utmost care they wormed their way silently across the shallow crater, and then swallowing hard Mason inched his head over the top. A single sound would now be enough to draw a burst of fire that could not fail to score a hit, but Mason could only pray that the Chinese gunner was patiently awaiting the signal of the next shell bursts and would hear nothing to tempt him in the meantime. Slowly the Intelligence man drew his body out on to the level earth, and then he lay there to shield Karen as she gingerly wriggled up beside him. So far they had maintained absolute silence, shrouded by darkness and smoke, and their lives depended upon continuing that absolute silence as they began to squirm away. They moved as though the ground below them was coated with eggshell ice over a pool of vitriol acid.

And then Mason's biggest fear was realized, and while they were still only a yard away from the marked target of their deserted refuge the heavy artillery behind the Chinese lines flung out another roaring cannonade. Instantly the Indian troops to their right and left opened up with covering fire, and the Chinese guns concentrated murderously on the shallow depression they had just left.

Mason was thrusting forward at the first crack of the big guns, dragging Karen on her knees as the machine-guns sprayed around their heels. Then she was up beside him and they were both running. Shells burst with an ear-splitting fury on either side and curtains of flying earth enveloped them as they ran. They twisted in the direction of the Indian battle lines and sprinted the last hundred yards as they had never sprinted before. The Chinese gunners hunted them blindly through the heat and sound blasted arena and it seemed that hell itself had burst upwards through the battle-scarred earth.

Then suddenly they were clear of the flying dirt and stones from the shell bursts and a barking voice rose up immediately in front of them and ordered them to stop. Mason stumbled and almost fell, but managed to bring himself to a halt a split second before a vague shape jabbed a rifle barrel against his chest. He saw the outline of a turbaned head in the gloom and knew that it could only be one of the Sikh troops. Karen blurted a stream of gasping words to identify them and slowly the gun was lowered. Instructions were hissed feverishly and two more Sikhs appeared to lead them back through the front line positions.

It was several moments before Mason realized that there was a third man in front of their two-man escort, but the man did not speak until they were well clear of the battle area, then he turned to face them. He peered closely at their faces in the gloom and then returned his cocked revolver to its holster.

"So it is Captain Mason and Doctor Langford," he said smiling. "I am Captain Balakrishna. I — I am sorry for — " He stopped and resorted to Hindi to speak to Karen.

She turned to Mason and translated.

"Captain Balakrishna does not speak English, Paul. But he apologizes for keeping us waiting out there. He thought at first that it was some trick of the Chinese. Fortunately he remembers us from the officers' mess at Tagantse, and as Panjit Sangh was with us at the time he knew that the Lieutenant was your aide. He asked about Sangh simply to check your identity."

"A sensible precaution," Mason admitted, and despite his aggravation in the crater he smiled gratefully at the Captain now.

Karen conversed with Balakrishna for a few moments and then the Indian nodded briefly and turned to give orders to his two men. Karen turned back to Mason.

"He says that we'll have to walk a couple of miles before we can reach the road, but there we might be lucky and find some transport going to Tagantse.

With a battle imminent it's the best he can do, but he's sending the Sikhs to guide us."

Mason smiled wearily, and consoled himself with the thought that after crossing the Chinese lines nothing else could be quite so bad.

"We'll make it," he said. "Didn't I tell you so at the start."

And then even Karen smiled faintly.

★ ★ ★

Three hours later, after a gruelling tramp, an hour's wait, and finally flagging down a hurrying troop lorry returning empty from the front, they arrived back at the Indian Command Headquarters at Tagantse. They were tired, weak and bruised after their ordeal, and in many places they were still bleeding beneath their clothes, but Mason was determined to make his report immediately and Karen equally determinedly went with him.

They were delayed for several minutes in one of the outer rooms of the commandeered farmhouse, and then they were again received into the inner sanctum where Colonel Samdar Rao had installed his maps and files and all the other necessities of modern warfare. The room was now lit by naked bulbs from a generator chugging away in an outer barn and six or seven senior staff officers were lounging in different corners. Among therm was Major Radhaven who stood by Samdar Rao's desk. There was a strange, hushed air of waiting in the room, something that Mason could not quite define, except that it was not the usual tense atmosphere of a front line headquarters on the edge of a major battle. He sensed an undercurrent of feeling that was again impossible to define. Then the dapper little Colonel complimented him upon his narrow escape from the Chinese and asked for his report. Mason launched into the story while Karen, seeming slightly awed by so many high-brass soldiers in their own holy of holies, stood silently behind him.

"So the monks of Karakhor were behind this business of supplying arms,"

Samdar Rao commented when Mason had finished. Then his thin shoulders shrugged helplessly. "But that hardly seems to matter now. The monastery is behind the Chinese lines and there is nothing that we can do about it."

Mason had to admit that this was so, but pressed on hopefully. "But, Colonel, if your troops win this coming battle and push the Chinese back then the monastery will return to Indian hands. Some action will have to be taken then."

Samdar Rao pressed his hands flat on his desk and looked up into Mason's face with a forced, bitter smile.

"Captain, we are hoping that there will be no battle. Today Peking staggered the world by announcing that her army would honour a cease fire along the whole length of the frontier as from midnight tonight. Midnight was two hours ago, shortly after you passed through their lines. The artillery assault stopped at twelve fifteen and so far there are no signs of their troops following it up."

Mason stared, and slowly it dawned on him that there had been no heavy thunder from the battlefront since he and Karen had followed their two-man escort through the rearguard of the Indian lines, but until now the fact had failed to register through the combination of mental and bodily weariness.

He said slowly: "But that doesn't make sense. Why would the Chinese cause a halt to a war that they are winning?"

"There are two reasons," Samdar Rao answered. "One is that the Russians may have interfered behind the scenes. Moscow is in a position to exert severe economic pressure on China and may have threatened to do so to preserve world peace. And two is that the Chinese themselves must realize that to thrust too far into the heart of India will mean that the western powers will ultimately come to our aid. The cease fire terms stipulate that both sides must retreat twelve miles from their present positions, but even a twelve mile retreat will leave the Chinese in control of an area of Indian land the size of your British country of Scotland which they have seized since this war began. With that, for the time being, they will be satisfied."

"But surely you don't have to accept those terms," Karen blurted with unexpected passion.

"But we do," Samdar Rao told her bitterly. "In most places our troops are in retreat and badly disorganized. We could not stop the Chinese avalanche from breaking out across the Assam plains if the war continued. Even here at Tagantse we are on the point of wholesale evacuation. The fact is that this war is lost. We have been beaten by superior forces. The Chinese have grabbed a large chunk of India, and now they tell us that as long as we do not argue to get it back they will not steal any more. It is humiliating to accept but there is nothing that we can do about it."

Mason was beginning to understand the lack of activity and the silent tension of the room. He said quietly:

"So now you can only wait — and hope that the Chinese will keep their word?"

Samdar Rao nodded dully. "My troop commanders have received instructions to do absolutely nothing that could antagonize the Chinese, and all patrols have been withdrawn. It would be disastrous at this stage for some blundering skirmish to start the battle off again. The Chinese need only the slightest excuse to argue self-defence or provocation and their army will be swarming deeper into India and it will be impossible to hold them back." His face creased into sunken lines as he finished. "They do not fear the Indian Army, and with an arguable excuse for further invasion it is possible that they will defy the opinions of Russia and the free world. We dare not risk such an excuse."

There was a long moment of silence, and Mason felt vaguely uncomfortable at being forced to witness the defeat of the men around him. Then Karen broke the awkward pause.

"So we never will know what is going on at Karakhor," she ventured slowly, and her tone betrayed some of the frustration and bitterness she felt for all that she and Mason had been through during the past thirty six hours.

"It appears so," Samdar Rao admitted, and again he shrugged.

Then he remembered something and reached into the drawer of his desk, selecting a slip of yellow paper that he passed across to Mason.

"I must apologize, Captain. But this radio signal was received here this morning. With so many other things to worry about I am afraid that it slipped my mind until just now." He paused and smiled faintly. "I think that it terminates your mission here anyway."

The wording was very brief and Mason read it through slowly. The two hauls of British arms stolen from Hong Kong had been recovered from a warehouse in Kowloon prior to shipment to Indonesia and eight men had been arrested by naval police. One of them had been charged with the murder of the rating who had died on guard duty during the first raid. The second paragraph went on to say that the investigating officers had also obtained definite leads that would enable them to pick up the men responsible for the Singapore arms theft within the next twenty-four hours. It was now known that the Singapore arms had also been intended for Indonesia before an unknown buyer had offered double their value to have them shipped to India. The signal concluded that unless there was a definite hope of recovering the small percentage of arms still unaccounted for then Mason should return to Hong Kong. It was signed by Lieutenant Commander Alan Kendall.

Mason looked up and Samdar Rao said bluntly:

"It looks as though your Naval Intelligence is satisfied with breaking up the gun runners and recovering the bulk of their lost arms. They are not so interested in the mystery buyer here in the Himalayas." He paused, and then smiled to take the rebuke out of his tone. "But I think they are wise, Captain. Your task here is hopeless now that the Chinese have over-run Karakhor and are breathing down our necks here at Tagantse, and your seniors are obviously aware of the danger you so narrowly escaped this morning. If the Chinese had succeeded in holding you then Peking would soon have been screaming her old tune of British Imperialist intervention in Asian affairs, and that would have been embarrassing for the British Navy. It is best that you return to Hong Kong."

Mason had to agree with the little Colonel's reasoning, but it still galled him to think of leaving the job half done. Then, before he could think of some argument or new approach, there was a sudden disturbance from outside.

There was the sound of a jeep skidding to a halt, the engine left running, and then a startled exclamation of alarm from the outer room. Samdar Rao stiffened behind his desk as he stared towards the door, and the surrounding staff officers followed his gaze. Both Mason and Karen turned with them as the sound of raised voices clamoured from beyond the door, and the sharp-faced Major Radhaven felt tentatively towards his revolver as he took a pace towards it. Then the door was abruptly pushed open and there was a shocked silence as Lieutenant Panjit Sangh appeared in the doorway.

The silence was broken by Karen Langford's muffled scream, and then the young Lieutenant stumbled forwards into the room. Red blood smothered his hand where it was pressed against his left collar bone and the front of his tunic was soaked with dark, glistening scarlet. His face was sick with pain.

For a moment he held himself perfectly erect, and spoke very clearly and precisely, spacing each word.

"Colonel Rao, sir, I have to report that the village men of Ladrung have received new arms. And they are planning another ambush against the Chinese."

And then his knees buckled and only the swift movements of Radhaven and another officer prevented him from crashing to the floor.

17

The Flight of the Whirlwind

There was an instant of stunned silence after Panjit Sangh had delivered his shock announcement, and all eyes stared towards him as he was supported by Radhaven and his companion. Sangh's head had slumped forward on his chest and slowly his hand slipped away from his wound and hung limp. Then Karen recovered from the shock and moved towards them. The young Lieutenant was lowered to the floor and she swiftly knelt beside him, her fingers steady as she pulled open the buttons of the soiled tunic.

Samdar Rao had slowly gone white around the lips and nostrils, and now he straightened up behind his desk like a stiff-jointed centenarian.

"This is disastrous. If those blind fools start shooting at the Chinese it will ruin everything. It will be a violation of the cease fire agreement. It could mean — " He gripped his emotions sharply and his tone became one of command. "Major Radhaven, take a patrol out to Ladrung immediately. We must stop this ambush."

Radhaven saluted in acknowledgement, spun on his heel, and vanished through the door in the space of seconds.

Paul Mason took the Major's place and knelt by Sangh as Karen opened up the young Lieutenant's tunic. There was a bullet hole just beneath the left collar bone that was still bleeding badly and his shirt was sodden. Karen reached to tear the shirt away and then Sangh groaned and half opened his eyes. Mason's hand closed on Karen's wrist.

"Hold it," he said. "Don't touch him. He's still conscious." A flame of professional anger flared in her eyes and she opened her mouth to protest. "This is important," he insisted. "We must know what happened at Ladrung. If you touch that wound he'll pass out."

She hesitated and he thrust on swiftly. "Those hill villagers will not only start up a war again if they attack the Chinese, they'll get themselves massacred as well. With the Chinese army so closely packed and keyed-up for a battle they won't have a hope in hell of slipping away successfully like they've done before."

Karen drew a long breath, and then nodded slowly. She left the wound and supported Sangh's head instead, speaking softly to bring him round. Sangh's eyes slowly opened and the once-handsome face grimaced with pain.

"Lieutenant," Mason's voice was low but urgent. "Try and tell us what happened."

Sangh gritted his teeth and then said weakly: "I was looking for you, Captain. I drove to Ladrung and arrived just after dark. The village men were all gathered in a large group, holding a meeting I thought. But I did not realize until I had left my jeep and walked towards them that there was a monk addressing the meeting. A monk from Karakhor."

He paused for breath but no one rushed him. Samdar Rao had left his desk to join them and the remaining staff officers listened in silence. Karen glanced up and sent one of the younger men for the Army Medical Officer and a stretcher while they waited. Then Sangh began again.

"The monk was issuing Tarong and his villagers with more rifles, and goading them to more violence. It was too late for me to retreat for reinforcements, and so I tried to argue with Tarong. But they would not listen and then — " He made another grimace of pain. "And then the monk simply shot me.

"When I recovered consciousness the monk and all the men from the village had gone. I was lying against the wall of one of the houses and they must have thought that I was dead. I got up and found one of the women. She said that the men had followed the monk and that they were going to kill more Chinese — but she would not say where. I managed to get back to my jeep then and drove here to Tagantse."

Mason pictured the killing agony of driving the jeep through the night, with every jolt aggravating the bleeding as it tore at the ugly bullet wound, and the thought made him wince. He said quietly: "Thanks, Lieutenant. You did a damned good job." And then he nodded at Karen to continue. She pulled the blood-soaked shirt from the wound and Panjit Sangh fainted away.

Samdar Rao looked grim and caught the attention of one of his junior officers. "Catch up with Major Radhaven," he ordered. "And give him the full details of Lieutenant Sangh's report. And see that a warning is passed to all troop commanders in the Ladrung area."

The man nodded and darted out as the camp Medical Officer came hurrying in. Mason relinquished his place by Sangh's side and rose to face the dapper little Colonel.

"What are the chances?" he asked. "Will those village men be intercepted in time?"

Samdar Rao looked haggard. "Possibly — if Major Radhaven can get the women of Ladrung to talk."

Mason recalled the sullen, unco-operative faces from his two visits to the village, and his face became grim.

"Then the chances are pretty poor."

Samdar Rao was forced to agree, then he argued defensively. "But what else can I do? Apart from ordering Radhaven to torture those women into submission. And even if I went so far as that the odds are that their men have told them nothing."

Mason said flatly: "There is another way. The monks of Karakhor are behind all this, and if they gave the orders then they will know where the ambush is to take place." He drew a determined breath and plunged on. "When I first arrived here six days ago I noticed a helicopter parked behind a line of Dakotas on the airstrip. That chopper could get me back over the Chinese lines and drop me close to Karakhor in half an hour. Give me a radio set to get the information back and we might still be in time."

The Indian stared. "The helicopter is still there. But how will you get inside the monastery?"

"I'll manage." Mason was coldly confident. "The walls won't be difficult

306

to climb, and the first monk I meet will get a gun barrel rammed so far down his throat that he'll be glad to take me to his mysterious Abbot."

Karen had straightened up slowly as they talked, leaving Panjit Sangh to the care of the army doctor and staring at Mason's face. Now she gripped his arm and said anxiously:

"Paul, you can't be serious. You're not fit to go back there."

"Doctor Langford is right," Samdar Rao agreed. "Besides, this is not your task and officially you have been recalled back to your base in Hong Kong." He paused. "I am sorry, Captain, but I cannot let you take the risk."

"Colonel Rao." The speaker was one of the junior staff officers, a second Lieutenant who took an eager step forwards, his shoulders bracing to attention. "Allow me to volunteer, sir. With a small patrol I can force an entry into the monastery and find out the information we need."

Samdar Rao shook his head. "Impossible, Lieutenant. A patrol will be more easily intercepted by the Chinese, and any fighting must be avoided at all costs. That is the blunder we are trying to prevent."

"Exactly." Mason forced their attention back where he wanted it. "This will have to be a one man job, done as much by stealth as by force. And I'm the only man who knows the terrain."

Samdar Rao studied the hard blue eyes of the man before him, and then slowly he nodded. "All right, Captain Mason. I'll give you your radio set and your helicopter. But you can't go alone. This mission calls for two men at least."

It was Mason's turn to hesitate, but quite suddenly he knew exactly who he wanted behind him. "It's a bargain," he said. "But can I request my man?"

Samdar Rao nodded.

Mason was aware of the eagerness of the young Second Lieutenant, and for a moment he regretted that he had to disillusion the boy. "I'd like to borrow Major Radhaven's Sergeant," he said. "The big Sikh, Marijani."

Samdar Rao nodded again, and gave

the necessary orders.

Fifteen minutes later the helicopter dropped out of the black void of the night, coming to rest on a clear patch of ground behind Tagantse. The great twenty-five foot rotor blades continued to spin noisily and their wind played havoc with the loose leaves and dirt that littered the landing site. An Indian officer rushed forward to give last-minute orders to the pilot while Mason paused for a brief handshake with Samdar Rao. The little Colonel's face was tight and strained and his grip was still hesitant. Then Mason turned and ducked beneath the whirling blades to climb into the fat belly of the helicopter. Close at his heels moved the solid, reassuring bulk of Sergeant Marijani.

The helicopter lifted off again with a minimum of delay, her lights fully blacked out as she headed towards Ladrung. Mason swallowed hard and reviewed his hasty plan of action.

The helicopter was a Westland Whirlwind with a range of three hundred miles and a top speed of over one hundred miles an hour, and it had been agreed that they would avoid the valley where the mass of the Chinese Army was grouped and keep as close as possible to the mountain range above the road from Ladrung to Karakhor. There was plenty of cloud cover and in the pitch blackness and flying at maximum height they hoped to avoid any heavy fire from the ground. The Chinese would hear them of course, but at one hundred miles an hour they would be swiftly over the front lines. Mason and Marijani would be landed within reach of Karakhor, and then the Whirlwind would fly on over the monastery and attempt to find a landing place in the wild country beyond which was believed to be free of Chinese troops. After three hours it was to return and pick them up from the gorge behind the monastery — if they were there to meet it.

Mason had to admit that some of the details were skimpy, but it was the best that he and Samdar Rao had been able to thrash out in the short time available while the helicopter was flown up at top speed from the airstrip.

Grimly he moved forward to confer with the two-man crew and make sure that both pilots knew what was expected of them. The two Indians were both young, but at the same time appeared completely unruffled by the urgency of their unexpected mission. Mason repeated and clarified the instructions given them by Samdar Rao's staff officer and the Captain acknowledged them with a slight nod.

"We understand," he said. "Fortunately I have flown this area before so there should be no difficulty in landing you close to the monastery. But to pick you up again is a different matter. It will be daylight and the Chinese will be alerted."

Mason said bluntly: "But you know your orders. Pick us up if possible but take no serious risks. If we can't get down to the gorge without bringing the Chinese to the spot then the Sergeant and I will have to do our best to get out on foot."

"We will do our best," the man

311

promised simply. And then he had to concentrate his attention upon the controls as they climbed along the darkened flank of the mountain. They were above the cloud and it was possible to see the jagged teeth of rock below the whirring blades of the twin rotors, and above them gleamed snow and ice and the star-lit peaks.

Mason watched the ghostly, deadly beauty of the mountain as it swept past, and his jaw tightened as he pictured what could happen if the great blurred circle of the rotor blades was to touch that unyielding rock. He glanced down at the unblinking profile of the Whirlwind's pilot and tactfully refrained from bothering the man with further conversation.

There was an outbreak of muffled, widely scattered rifle and machine gun fire as they passed high over the extreme flank of the Chinese positions, but nothing that came near enough to alarm them. The helicopter flew dangerously fast and dangerously close to the mountain, but the short flight was swiftly over and she began to descend into the clouds. Mason resisted the urge to stay and watch, knowing that the two pilots needed no distractions during this risky manœuvre, and returned quietly to the main cabin.

The turbaned outline of the big Sikh was just visible in the darkness, and made even more colossal by the bulge of the radio transmitter on his massive shoulders. There had been time to give him only the briefest possible explanation of the job ahead, but Marijani had volunteered without hesitation and Mason was very glad to have him. Now the Intelligence man used the last dwindling seconds as the helicopter lost height to fill in some of the gaps in the Sergeant's knowledge.

He had barely finished as the co-pilot groped his way towards them with the news that they were below the cloud bank. The man deftly unfastened the clamps and pulled back the sliding door in the fuselage and the wind sucked at their faces as they knelt by the opening. It was still almost pitch dark and the Whirlwind's Captain was inching her down as gingerly as possible. Then, just beneath the spinning blur of the blades, Mason saw the vague, darkened silhouette of Karakhor upon the mountain's shoulder.

The blind descent was the most nerve-tearing point of the whole flight, and Mason's stomach felt definitely queasy. The young co-pilot was tense and tight-faced as he thrust his head down into the slipstream and searched desperately for the ground, and God only knew what agonies of indecision the Captain faced in his seat of sole responsibility. Only Marijani seemed solid and unmoved.

Then the co-pilot jerked his head back and yelled frantically in Hindi to his Captain. The helicopter instantly stopped losing height and hovered. Another shout from the co-pilot and carefully she began to drop again for another two feet. Then Mason saw the ground, only twenty feet below them.

At ten feet the co-pilot turned and gripped Mason's arm. He said hoarsely: "It is dangerous to get much lower. The ground slopes so steeply."

Mason grinned at him in the darkness. "Then this will do."

He gathered up his sten, crouched, and then jumped. He hit the slope with his toes and rolled, crashing sideways with a horrible, bone-jarring halt. The impact slammed every ounce of wind from his body and it took him several yards to stop his slithering downward progress. He got up shakily and began to climb back as hurriedly as he could towards the hovering Whirlwind.

Marijani was crouched in the doorway some five feet above his head, and Mason had to shout to make his warning sound above the roar of tile rotors. Marijani understood, and swiftly unslung and dropped the transmitter pack into Mason's arms. Mason caught it deftly and then stepped to one side as the Sergeant's huge bulk dropped down through the night. The co-pilot gave a farewell wave and almost immediately the Whirlwind was retreating back into the safety of the sky.

Mason hurried to help Marijani to his feet, and the brilliant white teeth flashed behind the Sikh's magnificent black beard.

"No bones broken, Captain," he said. "Not even a sprain."

Mason smiled his relief and then returned the radio pack which Marijani quickly strapped back upon his shoulders. Then they picked up their stens and ran swiftly away from the landing ground, knowing that the sound of the helicopter must have been heard and that a Chinese patrol could arrive at any moment.

18

Back to the Monastery

They had been landed on the slope of the mountain where it joined the shouldering ridge that was crowned by Karakhor, and it took them half an hour to work their way round to a position directly below the monastery. The terrain was steep and treacherous, and once they had to sprawl flat with darkness their only cover as a strong force of Chinese troops scrambled past, heading at a fast pace for the spot where the Whirlwind had hovered to set them down. They escaped unseen and continued on their way, but the incident caused Mason grave doubts. He had expected the Chinese to investigate, but they were well behind the front lines and he had not expected them to arrive so swiftly. However, it was now a lifetime too late to turn back.

The stark, black outline of the monastery

was more definable now as they stared upwards, much more than when they had first left the helicopter, and Mason knew that both time and darkness were running out. From what he knew of their previous tactics the Ladrung villagers favoured a dawn ambush when their victims would be beginning to relax after the long vigil of night, and that meant that he had no more than an hour in which to find out where that ambush was to take place and radio the information back to Tagantse. In fact, he had less than an hour, for he had to give Radhaven time to catch up with Tarong and his men and stop them.

If he had paused to appraise the facts squarely he would have been forced to admit that his chances of success were painfully slim. But the stakes, peace or renewed war along the whole frontier of the Himalayas, were too high to admit failure while there was still even the slightest hope. Mason was fighting against the odds but he was determined to see it through. And there wasn't a second to be wasted.

He turned to whisper a brief caution to Marijani, and saw the answering gleam of the Sikh's teeth. Then together they began the last ascent to the monastery. They kept low against the stony earth and covered the last hundred yards to the foot of the towering walls upon their stomachs, propelling themselves with swift movements of elbows, hips and knees. The monastery remained in complete silence, and there was nothing to indicate that their wriggling progress had been detected by the Chinese in the valley below.

They both risked standing upright in the black shadow beneath the wall, and Marijani watched the slope and the darkness of the valley while Mason's eyes ranged upwards. They had noted that the great wooden gates were closed as they approached, and with the Chinese filling the valley there was no doubt that the gates would also be barred. However, Mason was quite confident that he could climb the wall, and he had come prepared for the task of hauling Marijani's huge bulk up behind him. Round his waist he carried a thirty foot coil of lightweight nylon rope that had been provided by one of Samdar Rao's staff officers, and now he swiftly unwound it and then looped the coil in a more easily accessible position around his neck and one shoulder.

He handed his sten to Marijani, received a murmur of good luck, and without any further delay began the climb. The construction of the large stone blocks had again left deep cracks where the poor mixture of too much sand and too little cement had crumbled away, but immediately he pulled himself away from the ground he became painfully aware of a forgotten fact. His finger-tips were still raw and bandaged from his previous ordeal of clawing his way across the wall behind the monastery only twenty-four hours ago.

The returning agony made him grit his teeth as he again hung on his fingers, and the tears flooded involuntarily into his eyes. But the urgency of his mission could not be denied and he forced himself to go on. Marijani, who had seen that first uncontrollable wince of pain watched him anxiously.

Mason remembered very little of that climb afterwards. The wall was twenty feet high before it reached the eaves of the lowest roof level, and it became simply an eternity of dragging himself upwards while blistering fires seared at his fingers. The rough stone rasped at his face and the world was all darkness behind his closed eyes. And then mercifully his hand encountered the slightly projecting eaves and he opened his eyes. His right toe found a foothold on the level of his left knee and with one last effort he thrust himself up and heaved his chest and shoulders on to the flat roof. He wormed his body forward and drew up his dangling legs, and then collapsed face down.

He lay panting for a moment, listening, and despite the throbbing of his fingers his hand felt towards his holstered revolver. But there was still no sound from the interior of the monastery and after a moment he relaxed. The flat roof on which he rested ran above the cloisters at the side of the black, square pit of the courtyard; to his right was the main gateway, and to his left rose the shadowed jungle of sloped and rising roofs and spires of the main building.

He pushed himself to his knees and crouched as he unslung the coil of rope from his shoulder. The far edge of the roof was crenellated where it looked down into the courtyard and he swiftly lashed the rope around one of the projections. Then he dropped the free end over the outer edge to Marijani. The big Sikh caught it as it flapped against the wall, and leaning backwards he walked up hand over hand. It took him only seconds to reach the flat roof, and Mason helped him to scramble over the edge. The gleam of teeth was again showing through the luxurious black foliage of his beard, and it seemed as though Marijani was actually enjoying the exercise.

Mason hurriedly unlashed the rope and recoiled it around his waist, for they could not be sure whether they would need it again. Then he accepted his sten from Marijani.

"What now, Captain?" the big man rumbled softly.

"The Abbot's audience room is on the ground floor," Mason answered. "We'll head for that and grab the first monk we can find as a guide. But no noise. If we rouse the whole nest we'll really be in trouble."

Marijani's giant hands cradled his sten as though it were a toy. "There will be no trouble," he said. "No trouble at all."

Mason grinned at him in the darkness and together they moved silently across the roof. They reached the end of the cloisters where the walls of the main building thrust even higher to the steep angles of the upper roofs and the delicate spires stabbing at the black night. Here they found a narrow wooden door and Mason pushed it gently. He exerted more pressure but the door was solid. There was no catch or lock, only a large brass knocker in the shape of a head with a long protruding tongue. Mason gripped the tongue and pulled and the door creaked softly and moved outwards. Carefully Mason inserted the snout of his sten into the narrow opening and levered the door open.

He moved inside into a narrow passageway, lit by the familiar smoky oil lamps, and guarded by the stone eyes of the statues of Buddha. The gross, fat-bellied carvings watched him from every niche along the walls. The door creaked again behind him as Marijani eased it wider to admit his huge bulk, and then the sound was repeated again as the Sergeant pulled it shut.

There was no sign of the monastery's inhabitants and slowly Mason led the way along the passage. His heart had begun to patter at a slightly increased rate, and he knew that despite the sten in his hands and the comforting shadow of Marijani at his heels the atmosphere had irritated his nerves. The inside of the monastery seemed even more smoky and gloomy than before, and the cold, eerie silence was too absolute to be true. The last time he had prowled Karakhor by night there had been the fear of discovery, but this time the fear was different. It was as though they had already been discovered, and it was only a matter of time before violence erupted all around them.

He tried to push the thought down, refusing to believe in sixth sense or psychic warnings, but his hands tightened on his sten nonetheless and he checked again that his bandaged forefinger was not too thickly shrouded to curl around the trigger.

They reached an intersection in the passageways and here there was a square opening in the floor and a flight of stone steps leading down. The Abbot's audience room was on the floor below and so Mason descended into the thickening darkness. Marijani padded silent as a monstrous ghost behind him.

Mason was just about to set foot on the ground floor passageway when he heard a sound to his left. His free hand gestured in warning as he moved swiftly back up the stairs, but Marijani had already anticipated him and was pressing back into the darkness. Mason kept his back hard against the stone wall as the orange robes of a monk appeared in the dim flickering light to their left. The man moved slowly towards them, his head bowed slightly in meditation. His long robes swished softly on the bare stone floor, it was a repeat of the sound Mason had first heard.

The Intelligence man smiled with grim pleasure as the unsuspecting monk approached, for here, whether he liked it or not, was their guide to the holy Abbot. He waited until the orange-robed man was almost level with the darkened stairway and then took one lightning step forwards that brought him full in the man's path. The monk's head jerked up in alarm and he opened his mouth to shout and started back at the same time. Mason effectively stopped both moves, his left hand clamping on the monk's shoulder to prevent his retreat, and his right thrusting the barrel of the sten into the open mouth to turn the shout into a gagging splutter.

It was almost too easy. The monk simply trembled in terror and stared aghast into Mason's eyes. Then Marijani appeared in Mason's range of vision, his own sten jabbing gently at the monk's belly and his big voice murmuring softly in Hindi. The monk gagged weakly and moved his head as well as he was able with Mason's sten boring against the roof of his mouth.

Marijani smiled. "Take the gun away, Captain," he said. "This one will give us no trouble."

Mason nodded and removed the gun.

"Ask him where we can find the Abbot," he said quietly.

Marijani translated the demand and the monk made a negative gesture with his hands. The big Sikh's smile gleamed again behind his beard and this time there was less restraint behind the jab of his sten. The monk winced and gave a whimpering answer.

Marijani glanced at Mason, his smile nicely satisfied. "He says that the Abbot is in the audience room, Captain."

Again the feeling that it was all too easy, but Mason squashed it down. He smiled approvingly in return. "Thank you, Sergeant. You take care of him while I lead the way. He'll give directions."

Marijani nodded and Mason relinquished his hold on the monk's shoulder. Marijani's big hand took his place and there was a further murmur of Hindi. The monk answered fearfully.

"Straight on, Captain," Marijani said. "Then take the second turning to the right."

Mason nodded and moved off, his sten once more at the ready. The smoke-filled air was beginning to work its way into his lungs again and he had to stem the need to cough and clear his throat. Behind him he could hear the faint rustle of robes from their unwilling guide as Marijani propelled him along, and the sound was almost a comfort. The unnatural silence was starting to give him claustrophobia.

They passed the first branching corridor and then turned into the second. There was another soft exchange of words that barely reached Mason's ears, and then Marijani told him to take the next passage to the right. Mason obeyed and after a moment he was sure that he recognized a particularly evil little statuette from his first visit. He was back on ground that he vaguely knew. Then he cautiously turned a corner and came face to face with something else with which he was familiar. The sour face of the monk who had been his reluctant and hostile host on his previous night at the monastery.

The man gave a frightened gasp, his body stiffening. And then Mason's reflexes flowed into action and he sprang forwards. The butt of his sten made a sweeping arc that started from his right hip and ended with a solid crack against the monk's jaw. The sour-faced man reeled against the wall and slowly slumped down into a sleeping sitting position on the floor.

There was another sound behind him and Mason twisted round, but it was only the recoil of their reluctant guide as he cringed in Marijani's tightening grip. The big Sikh glanced down at the unconscious man on the floor and then smiled almost fondly at Mason.

"Nice work, Captain. Very nice."

Mason grinned his relief. The encounter had helped to still the horribly uneasy feeling that everything had proved far too simple. He stepped past the sour-faced man and was almost grateful to him for restoring his confidence.

Marijani forced more directions from their now terrified guide, and moments later Mason recognized the door of the Abbot's audience room farther down the passage. He paused for a moment, picking out the nearer door from which the ape-like monk had appeared the last time he had been here, and the grotesque statue on the right behind which he had crouched in hiding. Then he moved on slowly, passing both until he reached the door of the audience room. He was relieved by the fact that there were no sentries outside, and reasoned that the guard must be maintained only when there were visitors in the monastery.

He turned quietly to Marijani. "Wait here, Sergeant. And keep a tight grip on our guide just in case the Abbot isn't here. I'll go in alone."

Marijani murmured an acknowledgement and then pulled his unprotesting prisoner back into the shadows by the wall. Mason took a firmer grip on his sten and then tried the door. It opened, and without any hesitation he thrust his way inside.

The room was exactly as he remembered it. The scarlet drapes on either side, and the golden drapes directly ahead. The incense still burned from the high pedestals in each corner. And the room was again empty.

The door slowly swung shut behind him as he stood there, creaking into place of its own accord. He stared round and for a moment he relaxed with the thought that their guide had either been lying or mistaken. And then he heard a rustle of movement from behind the golden drapes.

Mason's muscles stiffened again, and then slowly he moved towards the hanging curtains. He reached out almost hesitantly to grip the golden material, and then with a savage wrench he tore them aside.

He found himself face to face with the holy Abbot of Karakhor, but the creature before him was difficult to associate with the recognized human form. The man was a midget, barely four feet high, and looking even smaller as he squatted like an animal amongst the huge pile of cushions. His limbs were grotesquely deformed, and the head was shrunken to child-like proportions that looked diminutive even on that pathetic body. The freak's eyes were bright with evil, shining brilliantly in his tiny face. He smiled unconcernedly and spoke in the well-remembered squeak of a voice.

"Welcome again, Captain Mason. Welcome again. I have been expecting you." He chuckled at the consternation on Mason's face. "Oh yes, Captain, I have been expecting you for a long time."

19

The Power of Hatred

Mason felt the skin crawl on the back of his neck as he stared down at the warped figure on the cushions, while the calm statement that he was expected echoed with a note of warning in his ears. He stepped back a pace and glanced swiftly round the room, but the remaining curtains were still. There was no sound of danger, and no outcry from Marijani waiting on guard outside the door. Control returned and Mason lowered his gaze again to the tiny freak. The midget was still smiling up at him, careless of the levelled sten. There was no weapon on the cushions beside him, and no indication that anything was concealed in his vivid orange robes that hid both his crossed hands and feet.

The initial shock was over and Mason said slowly: "So you're the mystery Abbot of Karakhor. I'm not surprised that we were not allowed to see you before."

"But you are surprised now, Captain Mason." The squeaky voice was tinged with pleasure. "You did not expect your enemy to be one so mis-shapen and defenceless as I?"

Mason lowered his sten, realizing that for the moment it was not necessary.

"You are a bit of a shock," he admitted. "But what did you mean when you said that I was expected?"

The tiny face beamed at him. "We heard the helicopter, Captain. And then we saw it as it passed between the monastery and the mountain. I wondered why a helicopter should land so near here and then fly on into the wilderness. I did not like it, so I ordered my followers to keep watch. You were seen as you climbed up the wall. I knew then that you would be coming here."

"Do you know why I have come?"

The tiny head twisted to one side, and the bright eyes stared like pin points of rising fire. They regarded Mason for a long, silent moment, and the skin

334

became clammy along the length of the Intelligence man's spine.

"You come because you are curious," the Abbot squeaked softly. "You come to learn why I am stirring up trouble here on the frontier. You come to learn how I came to be Abbot of Karakhor — and why."

"Not exactly." Mason was suddenly aware that time was running out fast, and that the answers to those questions would have to take second place. He could not afford to be sidetracked from the main purpose of his mission. He went on bluntly. "All I want at the moment is the location of the ambush that the villagers from Ladrung are planning to spring on the Chinese."

The eyes sharpened and the midget hunched forwards on his cushions, his voice becoming dangerous.

"And what makes you think that I know where this ambush will take place?"

"Because you planned it. You supplied the arms — and one of your monks is leading it."

The Abbot beamed again, a happy,

child-like smile, and then the strange shrunken head nodded in agreement.

"You are right, Captain Mason. I am responsible. I planned it all. But — " A note of menace crept into the squeaky tone that so perfectly fitted the weird body. "But there is nothing that you can do about it, Captain. That ambush *will* take place."

Mason said savagely: "Do you realize what you're doing? There has been a cease fire agreement along the front, but if those villagers attack the Chinese along the battle line it will most certainly spark off another attack. And the Indian troops are not strong enough to stop it. You'll have caused the deaths of God knows how many fighting men and provided the Chinese with an excuse to thrust farther south into Assam." He stopped suddenly, and then said: "Or is that your intention? Are you working for the Chinese?"

The Abbot smiled. "No, Captain Mason. Perhaps the Chinese will be grateful for my intervention, for as you say it will give them the opportunity to claim that India has rejected their magnanimous offer for peace and become the aggressor. But I am not interested in helping the Chinese. Neither do I care for the cease fire agreement and the hopes of India."

"Then what do you care for?" Mason demanded. "Who can profit from this madness. Why even your own people, the villagers of Ladrung, will be massacred if they attempt to attack the Chinese now. They — "

He stopped there as he saw the abrupt blaze of hatred that blossomed in the midget's eyes. The smile was gone and the tiny mouth had compressed to an almost invisible line, the pathetic body was trembling with fury. Paul Mason stared, and for the first time a glimmer of understanding opened in his mind. He had sensed from the start that there was no motive of gain behind the mystery of Karakhor, but now the true motive began to unveil before his eyes. The power of hatred.

He said softly: "You want those hill men killed — don't you? You want every grown man of Ladrung wiped out in his own blood? You want revenge against a whole village!"

"Yes!" The scream shrilled into Mason's face, and the freak's hands appeared from his robes, the spindly fingers cupping like begging talons as he leaned forward. "Yes, Captain Mason. I want revenge. I have played the men of Ladrung against both sides in the hope that one of those armies would raze that village to the ground and kill them all. But they have been too clever. Tarong and his men know these hills and mountains too well. Always they have attacked and escaped. But not this time. This time the Chinese are massed too thickly around them. This time they must die. They must all die!"

Mason's hands had tightened around his sten again as the evil flood shrilled from the dribbling lips, watching as the fires of hatred burned like pools of hell in the brilliant eyes.

"Why?" he asked hoarsely. "What have they done?"

"Why, Captain Mason!" The madness had simmered slightly and the Abbot struggled to keep his squeaking voice

338

below the level of hysteria. "I will tell you, Captain. I will tell you."

A thin tiny hand moved to wipe the spittle from his lips as he regained control, and then he said bitterly: "I was born in that village of Ladrung, forty years ago. It may surprise you, Captain Mason, but I am forty years old. I was born, as you can see, with a badly deformed body — but not quite as badly deformed as it is now. I was a midget, but apart from my head the rest of my body was proportionate to my size. As you might expect, I was not a very welcome addition to the village, and if their religion had not forbidden it, no doubt I would have been speedily killed. I was allowed to live, but only grudgingly, and my only childhood friends were here — the holy men of Karakhor."

His eyes burned hypnotically into Mason's brain, and despite the fact that valuable time was draining away the Britisher felt compelled to listen as the hate-filled voice squeaked on.

"When I was twelve years old a group of travelling entertainers passed through Ladrung. They had dancing bears and jugglers and small side-shows, and when their leader saw me he offered to buy me to exhibit as a freak in his show. The villagers saw their chance to get rid of me, and although I tried to run away to Karakhor they quickly caught me. They laughed a lot at my attempts to escape and gave me away in exchange for money."

The little body was trembling again with fury but the brilliant eyes were still locked into Mason's mind.

"I spent six years with that travelling sideshow, Captain Mason, most of it tied into a wooden chair so that I should not escape. The marks of the string they tied me with are still around my ankles and throat. At the start I was beaten because I cried, so I soon learned not to cry. My body became even more twisted during those years, because a boy cannot grow without exercise and tied permanently to a chair. But that did not matter to my masters, for the more grotesque I became, the more people would pay to come and stare at me in the little tent where I was concealed.

"We travelled through China, and all over Asia, until at last we arrived at Hong Kong. Here the sideshow broke up, but that was of no help to me for I was immediately sold to a fairground owner in Kowloon. I was kept in another small tent for exhibition to the Chinese only, for my new owner, a fat Portuguese, was afraid that if my presence became known to the British authorities then they would protest and take me away. However, my new life was a slight improvement on the old. The Portuguese did not ill treat me without cause and I was given better food. I was even allowed to have books and newspapers that he had finished with and gradually I taught myself to read and learned something of the world about me. Because of my useless body, my mind, despite its small size, was much more active than normal, and I grasped things fairly quickly.

"But I was still a prisoner, and although I was no longer tied to a chair I was never allowed to leave the fairground tent. When the Portuguese went out he would chain my ankle to the centre post like that of a dog. My only friends were two wretched creatures who were exhibited in the two adjoining tents. You have met them both, Captain Mason, two nights ago at your billet in Tagantse. The man you shot was Torkal, whose body is covered with vivid tattoos; and the man with whom you fought was Chong, who has thick black hair like that of an animal from head to foot. They were billed as the tattooed marvel, and the wild jungle man from Cambodia. I was the living pygmy with the shrunken head. The Portuguese allowed us only an obscenely tiny scrap of rag around our loins and made a lot of money."

Mason remembered the powerful ape-like man with the monstrously hairy throat and hands, and swallowed hard as he realized that he had been fighting with a fairground wild man. He said hoarsely:

"But how did you get back here, to Karakhor?"

"Patience, Captain," the freak smiled evilly. "Patience and I will tell you all. I spent eight years in that sideshow in

Hong Kong, and then one night the Portuguese was drunk and careless. He released me from my chain and tried to force me to do tricks. I wriggled away and dodged through the canvas into Chong's tent where he was kept in a large cage of stout bamboo poles. The Portuguese came after me and the sight enraged Chong who reached through the bars and caught his throat. I ran over to the corner, I was terrified, and then I saw a large rusty spike that had once been used to pin the tent to the ground. I grabbed it, and while Chong held the Portuguese by the throat I stabbed the spike into his fat belly. I stabbed him again and again with all of my strength until the floor was red with his blood!"

The squeaky voice had gone thick with pleasure and the brilliant eyes had lost their hypnotic effect as the freak relived the moment with relish, his tiny hands clasped together in frenzied repetition of the act. Then slowly they unclenched and the moment was past. The boring eyes began to drill into Mason's mind again and re-asserted control.

"When the Portuguese was dead I took his keys," he said. "And then I released Chong and Torkal. We ran away from the fairground and then found our way out of the city. Neither of my two companions knew where to go next, they had thought only of getting away before the body of the Portuguese was discovered, but I was determined to come back here to Karakhor, and finally they came with me. It took us three years to make our way back through China, for many times we were lost and could not find the right roads. We made strange companions, each of us a freak of humanity, and while sometimes our appearance made people curious and begging easy, at other times they would drive us away with stones. Much of the way I rode on Chong's broad shoulders, for both he and Torkal considered that they owed me their freedom, as well as respecting my superior intelligence.

"However, after many travels and hardships, we at last reached Karakhor, arriving by night and avoiding that hated village of Ladrung. A few of the monks wished to turn us away, but the old Abbot remembered me and we stayed. He also respected our desire for secrecy in case more travelling sideshows should pass and attempt to kidnap any of us for further exhibition, and so for the last ten years nothing has been known of our presence outside the monastery. We were accepted and ordained as monks and lived the holy life of Karakhor."

There was a brief silence, but Mason was held by the fascination of the bright eyes in the tiny face, and he waited dumbly for the freak to go on. His sten had lowered to point to the ground and he stood motionless against the background of scarlet drapes and drifting swirls of burning incense.

The freak's eyes remained unblinking and he went on: "At the start I was satisfied with my life here at the monastery. It was a haven of peace where there was no one to chain me at night and no endless streams of peering faces and feeling fingers by day. And then there slowly rose to the surface the one thing that I still wanted — revenge.

Every time that I thought of that accursed village down there in the hills, and of the people who had sold me into slavery and degradation my soul would not rest. I craved to see them suffer and bleed. I craved it with all my heart."

His voice became bitter. "But there was no way. It was impossible. And so I continued my studies, taught myself English and widened my education. And all through the years the hatred grew unappeased inside me.

"And then — " The voice quivered with excitement. "And then suddenly there was a way. Two years ago came the first signs that one day the Chinese would support with force their claim that this part of India was Chinese soil, and that there would be war here in the Himalayas. I saw then how the Chinese could accomplish what I could not. I spoke of my plan to the old Abbot, but he would not hear of it. He was shocked and cried that I was mad. I saw then that he would not help me as I thought, and so I had to kill him. I added poison to his food.

"It was easy then to become Abbot in his place, for of course I had Torkal and Chong to assist me. The man who should have been the old Abbott's successor we also poisoned, and one or two others who tried to oppose my will. But most of them accepted me because of my eyes. I have very hypnotic eyes."

The freak chuckled delightedly as he watched Mason's face, and the sound and the boast made the Britisher suddenly realize what was happening to him. The sweat of fear seeped through his pores as he struggled to tear his gaze away from those piercing orbs and for a moment he felt that he was trapped. Then with an effort he brought up his free hand and clasped at his own eyes to break the contact. He twisted his head away and shook it dazedly, and when he looked again at the repulsive creature he took care to avoid any further direct clash of gaze.

He said harshly: "You're mad. Can't you realize that? Most of those people who sold you all those years ago must be dead by now. You're taking your

vengeance against the wrong generation."
He saw no response in the evil little
face and lifted the sten gun. "In any
case you're going to tell me where that
ambush is scheduled to take place before
it's too late. If you don't then I promise
you that you'll be just as dead as they
will."

The freak beamed at him. "But don't
you wish to hear the rest of my story,
Captain Mason? How I paid a Chinese
trader with gold from the monastery
vaults to act as my agent and provide
me with guns for my plan. It was the
guns that originally brought you here was
it not? Your stolen arms were meant for
delivery in Indonesia, but I was fortunate
enough to pick an agent with many
contacts and at the right price they
were very swiftly diverted here to the
Himalayas. They were flown to a spot
along the Brahmaputra river, and from
there Torkal and Chong brought them
to Karakhor on a convoy of mules. The
whole operation cost me highly, but there
was plenty of gold. The monks here have
been hoarding it for centuries."

The freak settled back complacently on his cushions and went on. "We armed the men of Ladrung and goaded them into attacking the Chinese, while at the same time Chong and Torkal attacked a few Indian patrols with some of the monks to make sure that the war kept going. It was all very easy."

Mason said savagely: "You have exactly four seconds to tell me where that ambush will take place."

He gestured with his free hand and snapped his fingers, counting aloud at the same time. As his fingers snapped for the third time the Abbot raised his diminutive hands in submission, interrupting him on the count of three.

"All right, Captain Mason, I will tell you. The men of Ladrung will make their attack on the Chinese at daybreak in a small ravine six miles to the west of their village. They expect to find only a small force of Chinese there, but in fact they will be facing treble their own number."

Mason relaxed, lowered his sten, and started to turn away. Then the creature on the cushions gave a shrill laugh and

349

shouted an order, and before Mason could raise his sten again the scarlet curtains to his left swished apart with one swift movement and he found the gleaming barrel of a rifle aiming straight at his heart. The orange-robed monk who held the rifle smiled at him coldly, and looked very competent. Behind him moved the hulking ape-like figure who had operated the curtains, whom Mason now knew was Chong. The fairground wild man was also grinning.

Mason froze every muscle, watching the rifle and knowing that if he lifted his downward-angled sten even a fraction then a bullet would crash into his chest. He silently cursed himself for allowing the Abbot's pretence of surrender to relax his guard, and slowly turned his eyes back to the midget's childishly beaming face.

"Did I not tell you, Captain Mason, that you were expected? Surely you did not think that I would receive you without preparation?"

Mason drew a slow breath, but said nothing. He was thinking that now everything would depend upon Marijani waiting outside.

Then the freak gave a mind-reading smile and chuckled softly. "Do not put your trust in the big Sergeant, Captain, for we have arranged for his reception also." And he reached out one shrivelled hand and pulled hard on a silken bell rope hanging against the wall beside him.

20

Massacre at Karakhor

The watchful Marijani grew gradually uneasy as Mason's absence lengthened, and his grip tightened on both their guide and his sten gun. He was tempted to kick open the audience room door, but there had been no outcry from Mason to warrant it and he had been ordered to simply stand guard, and so he stood his ground. He did, however, release the guide for a brief moment while he unslung the radio pack and rested it against the wall, for instinct told him that full freedom of movement might prove invaluable at any moment. He did not want his shoulders weighed down by the transmitter. He took up his grip upon the guide again, his fierce hawk eyes probing both lengths of the dim, smoke-wreathed passageway, and his ears straining to pick up any sound from behind the heavy, sound-proofing door.

Then abruptly the clear silver chimes of a bell tinkled through the silent gloom of the monastery, and instantly the big man was alert. His gaze flickered swiftly left and right, and then a brief scratching sound immediately above his head pinpointed a completely unexpected source of danger. His head jerked up and he made a desperate effort to twist away as he saw the heavy body dropping towards him from a square hole hidden in the pitch darkness of the high ceiling. Then the man landed full on his shoulders.

Marijani staggered, and then the captive guide wrenched away from him and grabbed at his sten. Arms locked around the big Sikh's throat and then with a bull-like roar the massive shoulders flexed and he threw his attacker aside. But another monk was already dropping through the hole in the roof and this time the impact brought Marijani to his knees. In the same moment more shadowy, robed figures rushed him along the narrow passageway and his sten was torn away from his grasp as he fought for his life.

★ ★ ★

Mason heard Marijani's first thunderous bellow and he knew that his Sergeant was under attack. But there was nothing that he could do to help. The rifle that covered him was one of the British arms that he had been sent to find and he knew that it was deadly accurate, while the monk who held it was undoubtedly one of those who had become well-practised during the ambush raids along the frontier. The combination could probably spell death at two hundred yards — at six feet it was an instantaneous certainty.

The insane, hate-warped child-man who was Abbot of Karakhor began to clap his little hands happily together.

"You see, Captain Mason. It is hopeless. Within a matter of moments the Sergeant will be subdued and your cause is lost. You must drop your weapon on the floor."

Mason hesitated, hearing faintly the

354

sounds of the raging battle beyond the door. While Marijani still fought there was still hope, but the monk with the rifle lifted it meaningly and bitterly Mason's fingers slackened around his sten gun.

Then two things happened at once, the distant sound of gunfire from the front of the monastery, and the abrupt entry of a breathless monk who burst through the narrow door behind the seated Abbot.

The new arrival gabbled a frantic stream of words at the freak who had twisted fearfully to face him, and then collapsed upon his knees, gasping wretchedly and wringing his hands in anguish. The freak turned back to face Mason and blazing fury had once again filled his tiny face, wiping away the gleeful pleasure that had marked his victory a few seconds ago.

"The Chinese!" He shrilled savagely. "They are breaking down the gates and forcing their way into the courtyard. They look for you, Captain Mason. They know that your helicopter landed on the mountain nearby, and so they seek you here at Karakhor."

Another faint crackle of rifle and machine-gun fire reached them from the courtyard, and Mason knew that the monks must be defending their monastery against the intruders. He knew too that it must spell the end of Karakhor, for nothing could stop the superior numbers of the Chinese now. By offering resistance the monks were committing mass suicide.

Again it seemed that the brilliant eyes of the freak had speared into Mason's mind to lay open his thoughts, for the tiny madman's body quivered violently as he thrust one accusing finger towards his prisoner.

"You caused this, Captain Mason. You caused it. Your presence guided the Chinese here to destroy my power and Karakhor. But for this you die. *You die!*"

He screamed the order in Hindi at the armed monk, but even as the sound was uttered it was drowned in a crash of violence as the outer door slammed open and the terrible figure of Marijani burst inside with half a dozen frantic monks still clawing around him. Like a lion surrounded by jackals the huge Sikh reeled across the room, and Mason roared a warning as the armed monk by the scarlet curtains swung his rifle to shoot at the new threat. Marijani heard, and twisted his struggling bulk with surprising speed. His great arms clamped around the throats of two of his opponents and hugged them before him in a living shield as he charged the man with the rifle. The monk fired two shots before Mason swung up the sten gun that he had almost released only seconds ago and cut him in two.

As the monk was smashed dead and broken against the far wall, Mason turned swiftly to aid the battling Sikh. For a moment the scene had frozen and Marijani stood alone. Both halves of his human shield hung dead in his hands. Then he released the bodies to the floor and again he flashed a gleaming smile, emphasized by the great black bush of his beard. He did not seem to have noticed the slight red stain at his side where one of the rifle bullets had passed clean through one of the monks at his feet.

Then there was panic as the remaining monks fought to get out of the audience room. Only two of them showed fight and those Mason accounted for with two swift blows from his gun butt as they faced him. Then, breathing heavily, he slammed the door shut again behind the last of the retreat and slipped the wooden bar into place. He turned back feeling temporarily safe, but he had forgotten Chong.

The massive ape-like figure with the flared nostrils and shaven head had moved away from the parted drapes to face Marijani. Both men were half crouching, their eyes wary and their hands apart as they inched closer. Marijani was still smiling, but now it was a respectful smile. Chong was unmistakeably enraged but again caution generated respect. Mason hesitated, but the Sikh's square shoulders were blocking his line of fire, and before he could move round for a clear shot Chong had lunged savagely forward.

Marijani sprang to meet the attack and

the two locked in a battle of the giants, Chong's arms crushing at the Sikh in a bear-like embrace while the Sergeant's hands sought for the ape-man's throat. They struggled and swayed, Chong snarling and grunting while Marijani gritted his teeth and fought in silence. Mason was forced to jump nimbly out of the way to avoid being trampled, and then out of the corner of his eye he saw the evil little form of the Abbot scuttling away through the door behind his pile of cushions.

For a moment Mason faltered, but Marijani and Chong were locked so close together as they twisted and staggered in mortal combat that it was impossible for him to risk using his sten until they broke apart. Then his faith in the Sergeant returned and he decided that the big Sikh could take care of himself even against Chong, and he turned to pursue the Abbot.

He jumped the pile of cushions and wrenched open the door that the Abbot had dragged shut behind him. Beyond was a small sleeping cell, furnished with mats and a palliasse of straw, the walls decorated by prayer flags and effigies of Buddha. On the far side was another door, still open, and Mason hurried across the cell and plunged through into a long passageway.

Here the sounds of the battle flaring around the courtyard sounded fearfully close, and he could hear shouts and screams and the yelling voices of the Chinese above the sound of the shooting. Of the mis-shapen freak there was no sign.

He hesitated, and then turned left towards the front of the monastery, guessing that the Abbot would be scurrying to join his followers as they fought to hold back the Chinese. Whether he meant to stop or inflame the suicidal resistance, or whether he simply wished to escape was impossible to tell. The only certainty was that whatever the urge that possessed him he would need the help of the fighting monks, for he was physically incapable of taking any action alone.

Moving swiftly Mason reached the next intersection, and there a sound to his right showed the unmistakeable dwarf figure of the freak running down the branching passageway as fast as his tiny legs could carry him. Mason raced in pursuit and the Abbot looked back over his shoulder and uttered a squeak of pure terror as he saw retribution looming behind him, and then he tripped over his own robes and fell.

Mason stopped abruptly, staring at the pathetic little creature as he struggled to his knees, and very slowly the Britisher lowered his sten. The mad Abbot of Karakhor was no longer a danger now, stripped of his friends and his power he was only a fear-crazed child for whom Mason could feel only pity. There was no longer any reason for pursuit, and whatever evil the freak had done he had paid for from the day of his birth.

The freak reached his feet, threw another terrified look towards Mason and again began to run. Mason stood still and made no move to stop him.

And then as Mason watched there was a sudden movement at the far end of the passageway, and instinct caused the

Britisher to press back into the recess of the nearest doorway as his sten gun again sprang to firing level. The fleeing Abbot was still looking over his shoulder as he ran and he was almost on top of the new arrivals before he sensed them and skidded to a halt. He screamed again and turned to bolt back the way that he had come, and then the savage chatter of a sten gun opened up and blasted the dwarf off his feet, bowling the already twisted little body like some grotesque ball along the passageway.

As the freak died the sound of laughter rang triumphantly above the fading echoes of the sten gun, and then the three Chinese moved out of the gloomy darkness at the far end of the passageway and came closer. Two of them were ordinary soldiers, but the man in the lead who had so callously butchered the defenceless little freak was a Lieutenant.

Mason's jaw tightened as he watched their approach, and although his conscience had suddenly acted to stop his pursuit of the Abbot he was more than tempted to exact vengeance on the pitiful creature's murderers. Then the officer with the sten gun reached the crumpled, blood-streaked heap and stared down curiously as he turned it with his foot, and Mason's muscles tensed as he recognized Lieutenant Sin Tai.

For a fleeting moment Mason's memory held the scene of Karen Langford standing stark naked while the Chinese sadist whipped at her flinching thighs and breasts with his brittle switch, and cold anger drained the last thoughts of a stealthy retreat from his mind. He could feel again the cuts and bruises of his own beating, and could see again the look of horror in Karen's eyes when Sin Tai had calmly ordered his men to rape her, and slowly and deliberately he stepped into full view in the passageway.

The three Chinese were still staring down with puzzled expressions at the corpse of the freak, and not one of them looked up as Mason cat-footed softly closer. Then he spoke Sin Tai's name.

The Lieutenant looked up and his slit

eyes went sick with recognition. And then with the greatest of pleasure Mason triggered his sten in a long, sweeping burst that mowed through the three Chinese like a swing of death's scythe.

Breathing harshly Mason stared at the scene, and then he heard the clatter of approaching boots and realized that the rest of Sin Tai's men must have forced their way into the monastery and routed the monks. And turning he raced swiftly back the way he had come, twisting twice until he regained the Abbot's audience room.

He burst in upon the last and ultimate scene of violence. The cushions had been scattered, the drapes torn down, and all four of the heavy stone pedestals had fallen to spill their burning incense over the floor. The dead monk whom Mason had shot had been inadvertently rolled from side to side and great splashes of his blood smeared the floor and the wall where he had originally landed. And in the middle of the carnage knelt Marijani, crouching upon one knee with the equally titanic figure of Chong stretched across his shoulders. The big Sikh held the ape-monk by the throat and knees and as Mason watched he slowly exerted the full hideous strength of his arms and shoulders.

Mason could only stare from the doorway; stare at the writhing figure of Chong balanced upon that terrible rack, his head hanging down and his open mouth screaming to the ceiling; and stare at the straining face and closed eyes of Marijani. The awful scene held Mason even more strongly than the hypnotic eyes of the now dead Abbot, and he could feel the moisture on his own back as he watched the sweat dripping from Marijani's face. He could almost feel every increased strain of creaking agony as Chong's back was slowly bended over those merciless shoulders.

And then with a final scream from Chong his back was broken, and Marijani slumped weakly as he allowed the now unresisting body to roll down his shoulders and flop to the floor. The spell was removed and Mason went to help the Sergeant to his feet.

"Thank you, Captain." Marijani's eyes opened and his teeth showed feebly as he swayed for a moment, and then the strength began to flow back into his limbs and the smile became more pronounced. "That one was a little difficult, sir," he said, almost apologetically.

Mason looked down at the Sikh's side where the red stain had grown larger and said grimly: "Are you all right?"

Marijani nodded. "Just a scratch, Captain. It's nothing serious." He became efficient again. "What's happening outside?"

"Visitors from China," Mason explained. "Someone was bright enough to realize that the only reason for a helicopter to land in this area would be an interest here in Karakhor. So they sent a patrol to investigate." He remembered their mission then and asked urgently: "What happened to the radio pack?"

"I was forced to leave it outside. It should still be there." Marijani smiled hopefully and then stepped over the body of Chong to unbar the door.

The passage outside was now empty, for the monks had rushed to join their companions fighting the Chinese. The bursts of gunfire were still echoing from the direction of the courtyard and Marijani lost no time in retrieving the radio from the spot where he had left it against the wall.

Mason grinned approvingly, and then suddenly the grin vanished as he sniffed at the air. He tasted smoke, but not the oily, ever-present smoke that wafted up from the flickering lamps, this was much thicker.

He said grimly: "I've got a horrible feeling that this place is just about to go up in flames, so now we've got two damned good reasons for getting out fast."

Marijani scented the smoke too and needed no further urging as he swung the radio pack on to his back and scooped up the sten that had been torn from his hands when he had been first attacked. Mason knew that it was hopeless to attempt to get through both the remnants of the monks and the Chinese, and so he led the way swiftly to the back of the monastery. He found the passageway outside the two rooms where he and Karen had slept the previous night, and ran down the length of it to the farthest room. Marijani followed him inside into another small cell, and through the open window directly ahead they both saw that the first grey light of dawn was already breaking.

Mason swore, but his stride didn't falter. He reached the window and leaned out over the sheer drop into the gorge, and saw as he had hoped that this was the nearest window to the corner of the monastery only fifteen feet to his left, and round that corner there was solid ground. He saw the first ever look of doubt upon Marijani's face as he looked into the gorge, and gave the big Sergeant a reassuring grin as he swiftly uncoiled the length of rope that was still around his waist.

He explained quickly as he worked and when he finally released one end of the rope through the window the big Sikh climbed out slowly to lower his huge bulk down. Mason braced himself to take the strain and gave a gasp of relief when the weight was removed and he knew that Marijani had set foot on the narrow ledge where the actual wall ended and the sheer rock face began. He risked leaning forward slightly to watch as the Sikh inched his way along the ledge towards the corner of the wall and firm ground, and he prayed the Sergeant would not slip. Marijani still held the rope but Mason knew that he could never hold that massive bulk if he should miss his footing.

However, despite his initial unease, Marijani turned the corner without fault. Mason breathed a sigh of relief, waited for the slight tug that was the signal that the Sergeant was firmly braced, and then he knotted the rope about his waist and began his own descent. Again there was the agony of hanging from his raw fingers, but he could only grit his teeth until his feet found the ledge. He moved along it slowly with his back to the wall and the dizzy drop starting an inch beyond his toes, and Marijani slowly reeled him in until they were reunited again on solid ground.

They lost no time in getting clear of the monastery, crouching low and keeping to the edge of the gorge as they headed for the main flank of the mountain. Behind them shots and screams still sounded from Karakhor, and with them the sinister crackle of burning as the first flames licked above the golden roofs.

They stopped as soon as it was possible, hidden by some boulders, while Mason raised the aerial on the radio and swiftly contacted Tagantse. They waited only for their message to be acknowledged and then hurried upon their way again. Around them dawn was revealing the mountains, gorge and valley, and directly behind doomed Karakhor blazed in fiery silhouette against the brightening sky.

21

The Balance of Fate

It was midday before the Whirlwind helicopter landed Mason and Marijani outside Tagantse. The pick-up had been made without incident three hours previously, a mile along the gorge from Karakhor, but as it would have been too dangerous to fly back over the Chinese lines in daylight they had been forced to detour west on a long, roundabout route that circled the mountain. The flight took them over some magnificent Himalayan scenery, but Mason was too tired to arouse even the faintest sign of interest or appreciation.

The moment the wheels touched down he forced himself back to life and helped the co-pilot to get the door opened. He turned then to help Marijani, who had weakened badly during the gruelling climb around the mountain and the descent into the gorge before the helicopter had picked them up, but the big Sergeant shook his head solidly. He had sat throughout the flight with one hand pressed to the large red stain against his side, but now he stood up and left the helicopter unaided.

Mason went with him to the Medical post, and assured himself that although the Sikh had lost a large quantity of blood his wound was not serious. Marijani smiled proudly at the report, sitting bolt upright in a chair and naked to the waist as the army doctor examined the puncture below his ribs. His white teeth gleamed again through his fine black beard, and when he insisted that he would be fit for duty again within a couple of days Mason could almost believe him. Then the Major who had come to meet their helicopter reminded him that Colonel Samdar Rao was waiting and he was forced to take his leave.

He found Major Radhaven with the dapper Indian Colonel, and five minutes later he knew that he had only won half a victory. His radioed information pin-pointing the actual site of the planned ambush had arrived too late for Radhaven to intercept the Ladrung villagers, and so Samdar Rao had taken the only other course possible. The Colonel had made radio contact with the Chinese and warned them of when and where to expect the coming attack. The move had stopped the ultimate battle from spreading and had saved the cease fire agreement, but it had also meant that the alert Chinese had massacred Tarong and his followers to the last man. The hate-crazed dwarf from Karakhor, now cremated in the burned-out shell of the dead monastery, had wreaked his vengeance after all.

★ ★ ★

Later that day he said good-bye to Karen Langford as he waited for the jeep that was to take him to the air-strip, and to the plane that would fly him south to Hong Kong. They stood in her tiny clinic and faced each other with an awkwardness that should have been impossible after all that they had shared together. Mason had told her all that had happened since they had parted, and she had told him that she had delivered another baby at Seral and that Lieutenant Panjit Sangh, although still unconscious, would eventually recover. Now they had nothing left to say, except about themselves, and both were reluctant to make the first move.

She was wearing a sarong now, a close, winding sheet of long green silk that heightened the smooth gloss of her dark hair. And he sensed that she had chosen it so that he could remember her more as a woman than a doctor. Her thin, gold-skinned face looked more beautiful than ever in the soft shadows of the small room, and her olive coloured eyes held his own blue ones with uncertain tenderness.

Slowly he lifted her hand, and as before he raised it and gently kissed the back of her wrist. It was the action of a dandy, of the Paul Mason who could only exist when the inner fighting man could rest. Without lowering her hand he watched